RETURN OF
THE CANOE
SOCIETIES

5-PATT

RETURN OF THE CANOE SOCIETIES

A Literary History of the First Nations' Coastal Tribes of B.C.

Rosemary I. Patterson, Ph.D.

To order additional copies of this book, contact:
Xlibris Corporation
1-888-7-XLIBRIS
www.Xlibris.com
Orders@Xlibris.com

CONTENTS

"Return Of The Canoe Societies" is dedicated to the many non-fiction writers whose works originally told the stories in the history flashbacks. In particular, thanks to: Jeanette Armstrong & Douglas Cardinal, "The Native Creative Process"; Harry Assu with Joy Inglis, "Assu of Cape Mudge"; Clarence Bolt, "Thomas Crosby and the Tsimshian"; Celia Haig-Brown, "Resistance & Renewal; Surviving the Indian Residential School"; Wolfgang Jilek, Indian Healing"; David Neil, "The Great Canoes"; James Sewid & James P. Spradley, "Guests Never Leave Hungry"; Daisy Sewid-Smith, "Prosecution Or Persecution"; and Paul Tennant, "Aboriginal People and Politics."

CHAPTER 1

Open Ocean

Despite the gusts of wind on the ocean that day the two elegantly decorated, ceremonial canoes set out for the waters of Cape Flattery at a lively pace. The paddlers were determined to quickly complete the first segment of their twelve hundred mile journey. The journey was a partial replication of "Qatuwas," the journey that the Canoe Societies had made in the Summer of 1993 up to Bella Bella on the rough coast of British Columbia to demonstrate a resurgence of culture. Taking part in the gathering were three thousand people from thirty First Nations Bands.

It was now the summer of 2000 and the replication of the original journey was being done by B. C. coastal tribes to demonstrate solidarity for their attempts to negotiate treaties with the Province of British Columbia. The opponents of the land claims process maintained that the First Nations peoples were so divided about what they wanted that the talks should be abandoned. To counter this claim, the present "Voyage of Solidarity" to Bella Bella by participating Canoe Societies had the support of nearly every First Nations Coastal Tribal Group in the province as it had already been over one hundred and twenty-five years since the first protest about the theft of Indian lands had been done by Coast Salish people in 1874.

Rachel McBay felt a gust of strong wind on her body as she paddled in the second seat of the first ceremonial dugout with dismay. "The forecast was only for a five knot wind," she thought. "This is much stronger."

Rachel looked out at the ocean as the twelve paddlers in her canoe, a black dugout with Raven proudly emblazoned on it's side in red and white, propelled the craft powerfully through the moderate chop on the open ocean towards Cape Flattery. She smiled as the enthusiastic paddlers from her host nation of the gathering, the Heiltsuks of Bella Bella, quickly pulled ahead of the second canoe from the Nuu'chah'nulth Nation, from the rugged, west coast of Vancouver Island.

"Make sure you're facing towards me, Darling, and look slightly to the right," Rachel McBay cringed as Nigel Kent, the strong minded, documentary director hired to record the journey, repositioned her grandmother, the tribal, ceremonial chanter.

"That's it, Darling," the handsome, middle-aged Englishman directed. "Perfect. Believe me, right is your best side, I know. We do want you to be photogenic, don't we? Now, don't move, not even a wiggle, unless it's a matter of life and death."

"As if we don't have enough problems," Rachel thought. "Giving the final say to the film director of this trip is going to be the death of us all. Nigel Kent is thinking only of the artistic merits of his documentary. And he's obsessed with reaching our destination at Bella Bella in advance."

"He wants to rehearse the entry of the canoes into Bella Bella, of all things, so that it's perfect in every detail, and time wasn't allowed for that by the tribal council."

Rachel braced herself as another heavy gust of wind struck the canoe.

"And now there's these death threats," Rachel sighed. "But that can't be possible, not in the Province of British Columbia." Rachel mused over her grandmother's words that morning.

"Watch out for any unusual boat travel, Rachel, anything approaching unexpectedly," Gran warned. "There's been death threats against the paddlers."

"Death threats!" Rachel remembered blurting. "Why would anyone be crazy enough to do such a thing?"

"There's lots of people that will do anything to stop the treaty talks, Rachel. Don't kid yourself. Believe me, what the white man thinks is his, he's not going to part with easily."

"What are you talking about, Gran?"

"Fish, lumber and mineral rights, Dear. Perhaps, even the right to Native self-government."

Another strong gust of wind struck the canoe.

"With winds like this, I don't think we need to worry about death threats," Rachel thought. "We'll be lucky to even keep this canoe afloat at all, without worrying about either death threats or getting ahead of schedule. And does it really matter whether the angle of Gran's face is photogenic or not, and which way the canoe should travel to shoot the most spectacular scenery?"

Except for Nigel Kent correcting everybody's positioning to get the best camera angle, everything had gone all right for the first day of paddling yesterday from the launch site in Washington State. But today as the canoes had started approaching Cape Flattery the wind had become downright dangerous.

Rachel felt ever increasing fear in the pit of her stomach as the paddlers pushed on. The strong gusts that were becoming more frequent and more severe were making moving forward at all very difficult. She stole a few second's paddling time as the canoeists regrouped to face the increased demands. Rachel used it to tie back her silky, auburn hair, the only visible trace of her great-grandfather's Scottish blood, with a headband.

"My God, there's whitecaps out there!" Rachel felt her heart rate start to thump as she stared out into the open water ahead of them. The waves crashed on flotsam and jetsam in the ocean as the canoe moved further towards Cape Flattery. The sun was high in the sky now and the foaming, salty, rolling whitecaps glimmered defiantly, reflecting the all-powerful sunrays.

"Will we even be able to keep this canoe afloat, Gran?" Rachel asked her grandmother, Martha McBay, as the waves started to crash heavily against them. The tiny elder dropped her photogenic facial pose and her rhythmic chanting and drumming at Rachel's question.

"That's a good question, Dear," Gran stared anxiously at the surging waves.

"Darling, you've spoiled that shot completely," Nigel complained as he lowered his video camera. The canoe swerved suddenly. Someone in the back had moved off centre and waves began splashing right into the craft. The water was alarmingly cold. Rachel felt more fear in the pit of her stomach as she contemplated the fact that the two lone canoes on the ocean that day were without an escort vessel.

"We should turn back!" Rachel found herself shouting. "We won't last forty minutes in this freezing water if the canoe goes over. Whose idea was it not to use life-jackets on this journey, anyway?"

"Wearing life jackets wouldn't be traditional, Darling," Nigel Kent answered. Rachel sighed as Gran abandoned her chanting and reached for something to bail out the water that was now splashing into the canoe with each wave.

"Use this Martha," Nigel handed Gran the traditional red bark bailer he had insisted we bring along.

"Didn't paddlers of the Canoe Societies of old use their powers with the sea animals and ocean spirits to control weather like this? Can't you do the same, Martha? I'd so like to get a shot of you calming the waves?"

"Some of the old ways have been lost forever, Nigel. Besides, if I were you I'd be more interested in bailing out the water around you," Gran replied.

"Mother Jesus!"

Irritation joined the fear in Rachel's mind as she thought of the reason she was sitting in the dugout canoe at all. Her grandmother's words several months before came back in full force.

"Your university degrees mean nothing, Rachel. The white culture has nothing to offer Indian people. There is nothing in their traditions that will heal us. All their psychiatric and psychological science gives us is diagnostic labels and mind-fogging drugs."

Sharp pain had formed around Rachel's heart at the words.

"You won't be able to help us, Dear, like you've hoped all these years unless you immerse yourself in the old ways. I know you mean well but as a result of your university studies, you've distanced yourself from your people and their ways."

Rachel had realised that four years of undergraduate and six years of graduate work meant nothing to her grandmother.

Fear increased as all the paddlers in the canoe became aware that it was possible that they were going to perish in the cold sea. The conditions were becoming even more dangerous.

"God, you could be snuffed out in no time in these waters," the tall, young women with the classical good looks of the Heiltsuk people started to go into a full-fledged panic.

Rachel felt the canoe come close to being swamped when a powerful rogue wave struck. The winds were getting even stronger. Gran and Nigel Kent were now frantically bailing out the frigid water with their traditional cedar-bark bailers. All the startled canoe occupants were desperately shifting balance each time the waves struck. The crashing waves seemed to come from slightly different directions each time. Rachel looked back at the other canoe supposedly accompanying them. The Nuu'chah'nulth canoe and the Heiltsuk canoe were scheduled to meet the Squamish Nation canoe at Port Angeles in two days to cross the Strait of Juan De Fuca to Sooke on Vancouver Island where they would be joined by the Sooke Nation canoe. The Nuu'chah'nulth canoe was a long ways behind them.

"I wonder if they will be able to even pick us up if we capsize?" she thought. The waves were crashing against their dugout canoe with a vengeance.

"We should turn back," she shouted again.

"No, we need to make time, keep the canoe pointing into the waves. We'll be all right," the Dugout Canoe Coordinator commanded. "The forecast is only for gusts up to five knots."

Rachel recognised another irritating voice.

"This must be a nightmare," she thought, thinking of the horror the canoe journey had suddenly become. If Rachel had known that Nate Archer, her long-lost, former fiance, was coming along for the journey she would have avoided it at all cost. A disabling mixture of emotions had surged into the pit of her stomach when all of his powerful self had turned up on the beach yesterday. Rachel tried in vain to separate her anger at his arrogance from the longing for his physical presence that had somehow never left with him.

"He's still hasn't changed," Rachel realised angrily. "Nate Archer was always ordering people around even back then."

Her thoughts went back to the day she had asked him to postpone their marriage until she managed another graduate degree. She had been granted unexpected entry into a Doctorate Program in Clinical Psychology.

"Another degree!" Nate had yelled. "You said a Masters degree would be enough, Rachel. Look, I don't mind you doing Drug and Alcohol counselling on the Coast of B. C. like you're determined to do. It should keep you occupied while I'm away at my job. But I'll be damned if I'm going to wait while you do another graduate degree. God knows how long that will take."

"It's an honour, Nate," Rachel remembered trying to explain. "I'm the first Heiltsuk female to be accepted into a Doctorate in Clinical Psychology program."

"Don't try to impress me with that prestige stuff, Rachel. It's money that's all important in this world. And you know I promised my parents we would be married this summer. They've arranged a huge Potlatch for us. I'm not going to disappoint them."

"A Masters in Psychology means nothing now, Nate," Rachel remembered herself arguing. "You have to have a Doctorate to be a registered psychologist."

Rachel had been so sure that Nate would accept it when she continued on with the Doctorate but he hadn't. "All of a sudden he turns up on the same beach I'm on," Rachel mused as Nate's voice directed the paddlers. "And he looks even better than he did four years ago. He must be working out. Nate didn't have a butt like iron and a six pack on his torso like a body builder back then. Life isn't fair."

"You wouldn't think Nate's present title as Vice-President of the Pacific Fish Processing Corporation would mean anything in this canoe," Rachel thought as he shouted out orders to paddle deeper and faster on the starboard side.

But the other paddlers instinctively followed Nate's order. The canoe shifted forty-five degrees to assault the waves head on. The canoe hit a huge oncoming wave with its brow and the vessel rose alarmingly in the air. It came down with a sickening crunch as the next wave was encountered. Some of the paddlers in the back lost their balance. There was an anxiety-provoking lurch to port and the canoe tipped.

"Mother Jesus, the video camera!" Rachel heard Nigel Kent shout.

"We're going over," Rachel found herself freezing with fear as she was thrown headfirst into the frigid water. She screamed as the bitterly cold water enveloped her. Other paddlers splashed around her yelling and clutching on to paddles.

"Oh God, Gran's sinking," Rachel realised as she felt herself going into total panic. The heavy, ceremonial robes her grandmother was wearing at Nigel's request were soaking up water and she was having great difficulty even holding her head above water.

"Do something," Rachel found herself screaming to Nate Archer who was swimming near her as Gran suddenly lost her battle and disappeared under the waves. "This is your fault. We should have turned back long ago."

The muscular, full-blooded man from the Heiltsuk Nation responded by diving down into the water after the older woman. Rachel grabbed onto the stern of the overturned canoe and fought to hang on. She sighed deeply as Gran and Nate Archer seemed to have disappeared from the world forever. Then suddenly Nate broke the surface after what had seemed a lifetime.

"He's got Gran," Rachel gave a prayer of thanks to the cosmos. Her heart felt warmth around it. She watched in deep gratitude as Nate pulled the ceremonial robes off Gran's shoulders and brought her over to Rachel. Nigel Kent swam over and both of them grabbed onto the canoe around Gran.

"Are you all right, Martha?" Nigel seemed very anxious about Gran.

"If any of us are, Dear?" Gran sputtered, looking at the raging sea around them. Other paddlers were frantically trying to hang onto both the bobbing canoe and their paddles.

"We've got to hang on till the other canoe gets here," Nate yelled above the ocean roar. "Or maybe try and turn this thing over." He motioned Nigel and Gran away from the stern.

"Oh God," Rachel gasped. Everyone was starting to flounder in the heavy surf. She and Nigel tried to hold Gran up. She was a poor swimmer. Nate and several of the men dived down under the canoe. Rachel could see their arms desperately trying to force the dugout upright.

"How can they hold their breath that long?" Rachel thought. It seemed like forever before the canoe slowly started to right itself. Then suddenly it flipped over. Nate Archer and the other men broke to the surface, gasping for air. The canoe was three quarters full of water but at least there was room to grab onto the sides now, although the sea seemed determined to push it over again.

Nate and the others crowded around the canoe, desperately grasping onto it's sides and trying to hold it upright. The men tried to splash some of the water out with their hands. Rachel realised the futility of their efforts. With every wave the water was more than returned. Nigel and Gran were now desperately clinging to the brow. It's carved head stood a couple of feet above the water and gave them more to hold onto. The canoe bobbed unpredictably in the waves.

Rachel stared back at the Nuu'chah'nulth canoe bobbing in the distance. It was barely making headway against the wind and the waves.

"I'm going for shore," Nate Archer shouted to the others. "I'll try and get help."

"You'll never make it, Nate," Nigel Kent warned.

Rachel felt sharp fear in her heart as Nate Archer ignored Nigel and set out for shore with a powerful stroke.

"I must still care a little about him," Rachel acknowledged. "He'll never make it in this wind."

The paddlers watched as Nate's head appeared between the waves in the distance only to disappear again as the huge waves struck. It seemed an impossible task but the Dugout Canoe Coordinator crept on against the hopeless odds.

"There's a boat coming in towards Nate," one of the paddlers suddenly shouted. "Looks like they're trying to pick him up."

Rachel's fear lessened. A boat far in the distance was moving towards Nate.

"It's still going to be too late for us," she thought. Rachel realised she couldn't feel anything in her hands.

"We're all going to perish," Rachel decided as she felt the growing numbness in her legs as well as her body.

"Gran's turning blue," she said as she glanced at her only remaining relative.

"That's not going to help," Rachel's still analytical mind pronounced, as she heard Gran start chanting an ancient appeal for help to "Raven," their clan protector."

Suddenly the canoe started to revolve in circles.

"My God, now we must be in a water spout," Rachel thought. The canoe started spinning rapidly. Those clinging to the canoe were thrown back into the ocean.

"Don't worry," Martha McBay shouted above the roar of the wind and sea. "It's Raven," she cried. "He's taking care of us."

"Sure," Rachel said to herself as the sickening vortex of dizziness increased. The canoe seemed to be spinning around in some kind of force field.

"I can't breathe," Rachel said to herself. A huge force of some kind was crushing her chest. She felt horribly nauseous.

"I'm going to black out," Rachel muttered to herself. Suddenly everything went dim.

CHAPTER 2

Potlatch Law Enforced

"What's happening?" Rachel gasped as she felt herself being furiously shaken like a rag doll.

"Rachel, wake up," some voice sounded irritatingly like Nate Archer's. It was giving her orders. She forced her eyes open and found herself staring into some still very attractive eyes that had taken years to forget.

Fear pounded in Rachel's heart as her thoughts returned to the raging ocean. She stared at Nate in shock. Then she gave a huge sigh of relief as she spotted Gran and Nigel Kent standing with his arm around her. Nigel looked completely dazed.

"Thank God you're safe!" she said to Gran. But then she forced my eyes to focus and realised that both she, Nigel and Nate were dressed strangely.

"It is them," she forced her mind to reason. "But they're dressed in clothes like people wore years ago." Rachel stared closely at her former fiance. He was wearing a grey flannel shirt, woolen pants and cap that looked like they belonged to the 1920's. Nigel was dressed in a black, three piece suit from long ago, complete with a tie. Gran was wearing a red woolen dress down to her ankles that looked like it belonged back in time as well.

"Stop that!" Rachel complained as Nate shook her furiously again.

"You've got to get up Rachel." Nate pulled her to her feet.

Rachel stared around at her surroundings. She gasped. A shudder of fear went through her. All three of the canoe voyagers were on an island somewhere but Rachel had no idea where it was. They watched as a crowd of First Nations people moved up from a collection of dugout canoes and boats with primitive gas motors pulled up onto the shore in the distance.

"Where are we?" Rachel demanded. "What's happened to the dugout canoe? Who are these people? Where are the others?"

"We're on some island, Rachel," Nate replied. "I think its off of Vancouver Island. I don't know how it happened but we seem to be back in time somehow." Nate sounded completely disoriented.

"Those are Kwakiutl and Heiltsuk people from another time period, I think. They can't seem to see us," Nate explained incoherently. "I think we must be dead or something."

"Don't be ridiculous," Rachel shouted at Nate. "There must be a reasonable explanation for this somehow."

"This is for you, Rachel," Gran said excitedly. "Raven has a task for you. He wants you write about your people's history, what they went through at the will of the white man's governments, both Provincial and Federal. So that the ordinary people of British Columbia can realise the truth about their government's actions against our people following the invasion of the English settlers. The ordinary person in this Province is not aware of what was done."

"What do you mean Gran?" Rachel gasped.

"You need to know exactly what happened, Rachel and to record the information into a book," Gran explained. "So that you and the people of British Columbia become aware of what our people went through and are still going through. What was done to turn so many of our people to despair, depression, substance abuse and even suicide and violence. Without that understanding, land claims will continue to be opposed and you won't be able to be the healer amongst us you wish to be."

"Don't be ridiculous, Gran," Rachel told her. Her Psychological training caused her to negate all that Gran was saying.

"You must be having hallucinations. And besides, I haven't time to write a book. I have to complete my Doctorate."

Gran just smiled knowingly.

"Come on Rachel," Nate ordered. "We had better follow those people, towards that village. I don't understand what's happening myself." Little of Nate's normal self assurance was present.

"I think we should go along with these people," he said. "Come on Nigel, perhaps this is the only way we'll get back to the others."

"They are probably all dead by now, Nate. I was losing my hold on the dugout, myself. My hands were almost completely numb."

"I know, Nigel." Rachel gasped in surprise as she realised that Nate's voice had real anguish in it. She realised that it was the first time she had ever heard him sound like that.

"I should have never ordered everyone to keep on. We never should have tried to make it to Cape Flattery in that unexpected wind. We should have turned back."

Gran put her arms around Rachel and hugged her close. Her eyes were bright with excitement.

"You think you know something we don't Gran, don't you?" Rachel said in horror. She was sure Gran was experiencing delusions.

"Raven's brought us back in the past for you Rachel," Gran repeated. "There must be something here, this day, that Raven want's you to witness and record."

"Don't act crazy, Gran," Rachel ordered. Her scientific training wouldn't allow her to consider what Gran was saying.

"How did we get here?" she demanded from Nate.

"I don't have any idea, Rachel," he answered. "When I came to I was lying on the beach just like you."

Rachel's head was reeling. Tears came to her eyes as she realised it was a good likelihood that their other companions in the canoe had perished.

"You're right, we must be dead, Nate," Rachel shouted in horror.

Even more villagers moved from their boats towards some buildings up from the beach. Rachel looked at the sky. The sun was just about to go down below the horizon. Her heart sank. She realised it was almost night. And they were in some place she couldn't begin to understand.

"Hurry," someone shouted. "The Potlatch is about to begin."

"Raven wants you to witness and record this, Rachel," Gran said with certainty.

"My God, she's hearing voices in her head," Rachel surmised. "The stress we just went through must be causing a transient mental crisis," she diagnosed.

Gran and Nigel started off after the villagers.

Nate dragged Rachel after them. Everyone was moving towards the buildings above the beach.

"That's Knight Inlet," Gran shouted, looking at the sea. "This must be Village Island. I was here for a Potlatch when I was a child. "But it looks like it did over seventy years ago."

"How do you know that?" Rachel demanded.

"Look at that longhouse," Gran pointed at one of a string of large cedar plank longhouses along the shoreline, "and that totem pole in front of them." A two tier ceremonial pole stood in front of the large house the crowd was going to. Rachel stared at the pole in shock.

"That's a Kwakiutl totem pole," Gran told them. "That's Thunderbird on top, and Raven on the bottom. And Thunderbird's wings are outstretched. Other poles, like Heiltsuk and Haida ones have the wings by the sides. I remember this pole. No one lives here now but Village Island was one of the centres of Kwatiutl life seventy years ago."

"Gran, you're only seventy-five," Rachel challenged. How can you remember this pole? You'd have been only five years old when you saw it."

"I remember it, Rachel," Gran testified. "Besides, there are many pictures of this village. But it exists only as a tourist centre, now. The longhouse, pole and school still exist. But these other buildings were torn down."

They followed the crowd. It was disappearing into a giant statue of Raven carved at the front of one of the longhouses.

"Mother Jesus, this is surreal!" Nigel gasped. He regained some of his ordinary enthusiasm for life as he stared at the totem pole.

"If only I had a camera?" he stated.

As they got up under the huge beak of the bird it opened suddenly to reveal a ramp.

"Imagine the bird concealing a hidden entrance?" Nigel exclaimed.

All four of them went down the ramp and found themselves in the insides of a large cedar plank longhouse. Totems painted in bright colours sat at one end of the longhouse anchoring the roof.

"Mother Jesus, the opportunity of a lifetime," Nigel moaned, putting his hand to his forehead. "And not a camera in sight."

"Where are we?" Nate questioned one of the revellers. The people all appeared to be in a good mood. To their horror the tall Kwakiutl man Nate addressed didn't appear to be able to hear or see him. Shock struck Rachel as she realised that she, Nate, Gran and Nigel were invisible and inaudible. Rachel collapsed onto one of the benches around the sides of the longhouse and sat down. Gran and Nate sat on each side of her.

"Christ, there's got to be a camera in here somewhere," Nigel muttered and disappeared into the crowd. An open fire was burning fiercely with smoke rising through the opening on the roof.

"Look at all the gifts for the Potlatch," Gran commented.

A pile of large, ceramic jugs, bowls and kitchen items were heaped in the middle of the community house as well as some Singer serving machines. Sacks of flour and Hudson Bay Blankets were piled everywhere.

"There's even a huge pool table, out there by the door," Nate Archer said in disbelief. "And a dugout canoe."

"Sad songs for the dead are being sung," Gran informed them. Rachel fell into a complete depression.

"Perhaps they are singing for Nate, Gran, Nigel and I, for all I know," Rachel thought. She had long ago lost any of the Heiltsuk language that Gran had taught her when she had raised the little girl in Bella Bella whose parents had died in a fiery car crash. Until a relative down in Vancouver had insisted Rachel board at her house and attend school in the city. Rachel couldn't understand a word the singers were saying.

The show started. Costumed dancers came out from behind a painted screen.

Nigel appeared suddenly in an open space near the others. He kneeled on the floor and started setting something up. Nigel had somehow located a camera and was setting it up on a tripod.

"Where did you find that, Dear?" Gran asked.

"It was one of the gifts for the Potlatch, Darling," Nigel replied. His eyes gleamed in the dim light. He disappeared under a cloth at the back of the camera.

"What's going on here now, Martha?" he queried.

"It's the Red Cedar Bark Ceremonies," Gran answered excitedly. "Part of the Winter Ceremonial. Watch for the Hamatsa," she urged.

"The Hamatsa?" Nigel questioned.

"The Cannibal Monster," Gran said. "He's returning from the spirit world."

"A Cannibal Monster, how photogenic!" Nigel was enthused.

"While the Hamatsa has been in the spirit world he's eaten nothing but human flesh," Gran explained.

"Sounds like WWF Wrestling," Nigel joked.

All of a sudden the sounds of fast drumming and whistles blowing filled the longhouse. A dancer came from behind the screen looking wild, dazed and totally out of control.

"The Hamatsa has to be caught and brought back to his senses," Gran explained.

The Hamatsa dancer was joined by four elegantly decorated dancers wearing huge bird masks. Their wooden beaks were over three feet long. Some of them even had movable parts.

"What are those, Darling?" Nigel's voice reached us from beneath the cloth at the back of the camera.

"Those are Cannibal birds, Nigel," Gran explained. A huge

flash of light lit up the Longhouse. Nigel was using some kind of flash powder to get enough lighting for his shots.

Loud chanting, fast drumming, and whistles all accompanied the Cannibal birds and the Hamatsa as they whirled around the dance floor. Then two other dancers appeared, surrounded the Hamatsa, and attempted to control his wild lunges.

"See the cedar bark neck-ring," Gran yelled to Nigel. "Once they get the neck-rings on the Hamatsa he will be under control."

Despite the bizarre circumstances, Rachel concentrated on the performance. The dancers were experts and Rachel realized she had never been aware of the complexity of the Winter Ceremonial.

"That's the Hamatsa's sister," Gran told them as a female dancer appeared, dancing backwards in front of the Hamatsa. "She trying to lead him from the Spirit world."

Rachel cringed as the Hamatsa broke free and suddenly grabbed something from down in the audience. It looked like a human body. The Hamatsa started to feed on it. A substance resembling blood started to ooze and pour from the body wounds. Rachel gasped in disbelief. Another bright flash testified to Nigel's fascination with the ancient ceremony they were witnessing.

Don't worry," Gran assured them. "That's a fake body. It's a dummy made out of bonemeal and red dye. The Hamatsa secret society dancers always were master actors, special effects people, and choreographers."

"Mother Jesus," Nigel replied. "They had me fooled completely."

"Really?" Rachel's university training still wouldn't allow her to accept Gran's explanation of the events happening to them.

"Sure fooled the white man, though," Gran laughed. "At the St. Louis Exhibition in 1904, Bob Harris, one of the Kwakiutl people, danced the Hamatsa and the European audience was convinced he had eaten a real boy from the audience."

One of the dancers held up a huge, ornately carved wooden rattle.

"Watch," Gran hissed, "that rattle gives power to the neck-rings." Before Rachel and Nate's startled eyes the rattle was shaken and the red, cedar-bark neck-rings were inserted around the Hamatsa's neck. The Hamatsa immediately stopped all his convincing resistance. He was led meekly off the stage.

"This is my favourite dance," Gran said as a group of completely different men took over the stage.

"It's the Klassila," she informed them. "The dancers are the Chiefs of the visiting villages. They're dressed in cedar bark headdresses with ermine tales and button blankets. They are dancing the Peace dance."

Another flash came from Nigel's direction. Rachel forgot some of her fear at the circumstances and lost herself in the show. After the Klassila, other dancers performed a Wolf dance, and a Paddle dance.

"I remember the stories of this Potlatch," Gran confided as the dancing ended. "It was referred to as the Potlatch of all the Potlatches. The one that Emma Cramner's family put on for her husband Dan Cramner on Village Island in 1921. Emma was returning the marriage security investment received many years ago in a Potlatch that was held when she and Dan Cramner were married, with interest of course. It's like a form of dowry. Marriage investment securities helped set up so many of our people when they were young. Now the debt was being returned."

Gran's voice sounded like she was very excited. Pain struck in my Rachel's heart as she worried that Gran was beginning to lose it completely.

"You should be worrying about how we're going to get back to the present, Gran," Rachel censored Gran's enthusiasm. Her psychology studies ridiculed trance states in aboriginal dances like the ones they had just witnessed.

"This rhythmic drumming, chanting and circular dancing is just inducing a trance. that's all, Gran," Rachel explained. "This is all like a mass hypnotic experience."

"How little you know, Rachel," Gran answered. "These dances reached audiences in the early days as far away as Hamburg, Germany. Dancers from the Kwakiutl, and Haida people toured Europe and even attracted Frans Boas, the noted anthropologist, to the northern coast to study our customs in the very late 1890's and early 1900's."

"If you say so, Gran."

"The ceremonial is impressive, Rachel," Nate Archer whispered.

"How ironic," she thought. "Our roles seem to be reversed. Four years ago it was Nate that devalued the Heiltsuk culture and now it's me that's equating the astounding performance in front of us to a self-imposed, hypnotic trance state."

"The women dancing with the Hamatsa?" Gran queried. Nate nodded.

"One of them was Florence Knox," Gran told them.. "That's Eagle down she had on her headdress. It represents the cleansing of the dark period of the winter ceremonial. The red of her button blanket represents the return of the spring, the return of life to this end of the universe."

"Sure Gran," Rachel sighed.

"Florence was dancing for her brother," Gran continued. "He owed Dan Cramner from another Potlatch. She spent two months in Oakalla prison for taking part in this potlatch tonight."

"How do you know, Gran?" Rachel gasped.

"See that man," Gran pointed to one of the men standing near a door. Rachel and Nate stared closely. The man was writing something down on a pad of paper.

"That's Kenneth Hunt. He's an informer sent here by Indian Agent William Halliday. He's recording the names of all the people taking part in the Potlatch and what role they are playing or what they do this night."

A flash of light illuminated the man as Nigel turned his camera in the fellow's direction at Gran's words.

Rachel stared at Gran in shock.

"The Indian agent turned Kwakiutl people into spies on others, Gran? And that lady was arrested, for dancing? I can't believe it," she commented.

"She and forty-five others, Rachel." Gran's voice got quite angry. "William Halliday, the Indian Agent for this area was determined to end the traditional dances of our people. Like so many of the whites he had no understanding and total disrespect for our practices."

"And the white government was determined to turn us into some kind of carbon copy of their people with their policy of Assimilation. Not to mention that the Provincial and Federal government officials were starting to fear our land claims. The fact that British Columbia was the only province where government representatives hadn't bothered to extinguish Aboriginal Title through treaties was beginning to catch up with them. Land claim discussion and strategy sessions occurred at the Potlatches along with other Indian matters."

"The white governments of both the province and the country wanted our culture and spirituality extinguished completely. And above all, they did not want Indian Land Claims being submitted to the Privy Council in England as the Allied Tribes of B. C. were threatening to do. Even then, some government officials sensed the possibility that British Courts would rule that Aboriginal Title had not been extinguished in British Columbia. That's the main reason why the Provincial Government enforced the Potlatch ban legislation in 1921."

"Don't get so angry, Gran," Rachel cautioned her.

"Anger directed positively is a useful thing, Rachel," she replied. "How do you think our people managed to get the Potlatch Ban revoked. It took several decades but it was revoked. Thanks largely to William Halliday and others like him, the Winter Ceremonial dances were silent in many of our villages for over thirty years."

"It was the same Indian Agent, William Halliday, that arranged the stripping of the forest on the Cape Mudge reserve on Quadra Island. Chief Assu wouldn't agree to one of the railroad company executive's wish to log the forest because he wanted the Kwakiutl people of the village to do it themselves. William Halliday, for a five thousand dollar bribe, took the matter into his own hands. When most of the Cape Mudge people were absent at the fishing grounds, he came in, got several remaining members x's and one man's signature on the logging agreement. When the Cape Mudge people returned twenty million board feet of their forests were gone forever."

"Remember the cedar bark ring dancers and the Cannibal birds?" Gran queried. Rachel nodded.

"One of those dancers was James Knox," Gran continued. "He was dancing with his two bothers. He was all of fifteen years old, Rachel. He went to Oakalla and spent two months in the men's unit along with his brothers."

"You're kidding, Martha?" Nate Archer commented.

"I wish I was, Nate." Gran's voice sounded choked, she had so much emotion in it.

"Don't take this so hard, Gran," Rachel advised.

"How can I do otherwise, Rachel?" Gran argued. "The government's actions here this night caused over six of the Kwakiutl villages to surrender their regalia, masks and coppers to avoid their people going to jail. The passing of the companion legislature to the Potlatch ban, the prohibition forbidding legal action for Indian land claims in 1927, caused twenty-five years of inaction. Our culture was given a blow it barely survived. And our resources were handed to the English invaders to benefit from while we lived in poverty. We were barred even from filing a legal protest, or seeking comfort or understanding with our healing practices, culture and dances."

Rachel was experiencing a deep conflict between her scientific training and her grandmothers words. In Canadian schools she had been taught that the Indian people had be generously compensated for the loss of their lands. She had also assumed that the vast Canadian country was largely uninhabited when the British settlers arrived. Rachel had been trained in university that ancient dances of aboriginals were a form of self-imposed, hypnotic trance. She had also been trained that the First Nations' traditional healing rituals were only effective because they allowed troubled aboriginals the opportunity for positive identity achievement.

"God," she thought. "I'm going to be experiencing identity confusion myself if this keeps up." Rachel had been thoroughly trained in the university enculturation of modern Psychology. It recognised only what could be scientifically proven.

At their end of the night Rachel watched intently as members of the audience got up and made speeches to Dan and Emma Cramner and another couple that were getting married that day.

"See that fellow distributing apples, Rachel?" Gran directed again.

She glanced at a tall man handing out bags of apples to guests.

"That's Moses Alfred. He served two months in Oakalla for giving apples to the guests." Rachel sighed. Nigel's camera fired again.

"And that lady. She's Mary Whonnock, the wife of one of our chiefs." Rachel and Nate stared at a tall, dignified lady who also appeared to be writing things down.

"Is she another informer, Gran?" Rachel asked, her heart somehow experiencing pain.

"No, Rachel. She was acting as the recorder of the Potlatch proceedings. Who gave what to whom, what speeches were made, and what quests took part in the Potlatch as cooks, dancers, ushers, etc. so they could be paid a small sum in gratitude. That service got her two months in jail in Oakalla as well as her husband."

"My God," Nate exclaimed.

"And that fellow there is Spruce Martin. He served two months because he gave a speech. Billy McDuff, next to him was sent to Oakalla because he went around to the different villages and invited people to the Potlatch."

As Gran spoke the walls of the longhouse suddenly started spinning. The spin quickly made all four of the paddlers dizzy and nauseous and they started to retch as their stomachs and chests felt like a ton of rocks were weighing on them.

"What's happening now, Martha," Nigel gasped.

"It's Raven. I think he's moving us somewhere else."

"Sure Gran!" Rachel thought as she felt myself flung uncer-emoniously on yet another beach.

CHAPTER 3

Harsh Sentences

The voyageurs never lost consciousness this time but it took awhile before their breathing and fast heartbeats got back to normal. They slowly managed to stagger to their feet.

"The camera?" Nigel was yelling at the others in horror. "Do you see any sign of the camera?"

"The camera was one of the Potlatch presents Nigel," Gran informed him. "The government probably confiscated it along with the other presents."

"Maybe you can reproduce what we saw using drawings?" Rachel tried to calm Nigel down. He was looking like he had lost his best friend.

"Drawings, Darling, why didn't I think of that?" Nigel looked slightly relieved. "Of course."

"Where are we now, Martha?" Nate asked Gran. He seemed to be convinced that she knew what was happening to us.

"It must be some kind of group hallucination," Rachel told herself. Her scientific training still wouldn't let her believe that Gran's explanation of what was happening to them had any validity.

Their eyes followed yet another group of First Nations people as they made their way up from boats at the beach.

"This isn't Village Island is it?" Rachel asked Gran as they stared at the group of longhouses stretched above the beach. They looked different. The houses were much closer to the beach and myriads of dugouts were lined up in front of them.

"I think this must be Alert Bay," Gran said. "That's where the sentencing was done for the Village Bay Potlatch offenders in 1922."

"Hurry up," someone shouted from the line of longhouses. "The Judge is starting the sentencing. Don't make him any angrier than he is."

The crowd rushed up to the boardwalk in front of the longhouses. The paddlers followed them inside one of the buildings. Rachel realised they were in a school of some kind. But it had been turned into a court of law. At the front a serious-looking man sat dressed in a magistrates robe. In his hand was a gavel. A pad of paper and a pencil in front of the recording secretary of the trial suddenly disappeared. Nigel appeared holding the pad and pencil in his hand.

"The opportunity of a lifetime, Darling," he explained as Rachel looked accusingly at him.

"Be seated," the judge ordered. The group of people around the paddlers went to the empty benches in front of the judge. Nate, Nigel, Gran and Rachel sat down at the back of the defendants but no one again seemed to be able to see them. Rachel touched the back of one of the people in front of her. He didn't respond.

"This is horrific," Rachel complained. "Nobody can see us, hear us or feel us." She felt her body feeling the prolonged shock of their circumstances.

"Tell Raven to stop this if he really is the one responsible," she ordered Gran. Her head reeled as she realised how crazy she sounded.

"Just pay attention, Rachel," Gran advised. "Raven is continuing your education."

"Sure Gran," she muttered.

A hush went through the crowd as the judge stood up to speak.

"As you all know," he said pompously. "Today is the day of the sentencing for the defendants found guilty as charged for breaking section 140, Statutes of Canada, 1906. Under this statute:"

"Any Indian or other person who engages in or assists in celebrating or encourages either directly or indirectly another to celebrate any Indian festival, dance or other ceremony of which the giving away or paying or giving back of money, goods or articles of any sort forms a part or is a feature, whether such gift or money, goods, articles takes place before, at or after the celebration of the same, is guilty of an offense and is liable on summary conviction for a term not exceeding six months and not less than two months."

"I have been informed by Indian Agent William Halliday that the officials of several Indian tribes involved in the unacceptable violation of Article 140 at Village Island on Christmas Day, 1921, have finally agreed to show remorse for their part in taking part in an illegal potlatch. They have surrendered their regalia, masks and coppers to Indian Agent Halliday, in lieu of a fine. These tribes include the Nimpkish, Cape Mudge, Mamillikula, Tunour Island, Fort Rupert, and New Vancouver tribes. To demonstrate the mercy of the Crown and to reward cooperation, members of these tribes will therefore be given a suspended sentence."

A large sigh of relief was noticeable in the room.

"However, as an example of the determination of the Crown to end the wasteful, detrimental impact of the pagan winter ceremonial dances known as the Potlatch, convicted members of other tribes who still show stubborn refusal to end their ceremonial dances will serve two months to six months of hard labour at Oakalla."

A gasp went through the crowd. As the voyageurs watched tears formed in the eyes of some of the defendants as they realised they were going to have to go to jail.

A police constable took over the proceedings as the judge left the room. Each of the defendants' names were called out and they were asked what tribe they were affiliated with. A printed list was checked for verification and the constable verbally placed each defendant into a line to the left or a line to the right.

When the constable reached the last of the defendants he ordered the line to the right to file out of the school room. The crowd watched as the members of the left line were handed blankets and told to sit themselves close together on the floor. "Let's get out of here while we can," Nate ordered as the one group of released defendants filed out of the door.

"No," Gran said emphatically. "Raven wants Rachel to witness what happens next and record it."

"For God's sake, Gran," Rachel argued. "Let's go. We need to try get back to the others in the canoe." She tried to pull Gran to her feet but she refused to budge. For an older lady she was ridiculously strong.

"They are safe, Rachel," Gran directed. "Raven tells me all the paddlers are safe."

"Sure, Gran."

"You go Nate," Rachel suggested. "I'll stay here with Gran. She won't budge."

"As you wish," Nate replied, looking upset. "I'll try and come back for you two if I find a way out."

"I can't believe that Nate Archer still looks so attractive," Rachel acknowledged to herself.

Nigel Kent sat transfixed. He was drawing furiously on the pad of paper. Rachel glanced over at the drawing. Nigel had reproduced a perfect replica of the Hamatsa from the Potlatch.

"That's exactly like the Cannibal Monster," she praised Nigel. "I didn't know you were an artist as well as a documentary film director." Nigel just nodded. He was completely absorbed in his drawing.

By the next day Rachel was wishing she had taken the opportunity to leave when she could have. Nothing had happened since except that Gran, Nigel and her had spent the night on the cold floor without even the benefit of the single blanket afforded the prisoners.

"The steamer's coming into the bay," another police constable suddenly came through the front door. Everyone stood up and they were herded outside and down towards the dock. Gran, Rachel and Nigel followed. Rachel noticed Nate Archer standing on the dock.

"What happened yesterday?" she asked him.

"Nothing Rachel. I still don't know how we got to this island or what the Hell we are doing back in the past. The people that came in boats went back to their homes, I guess. I thought of going with them but I didn't want to abandon you. I just wandered the streets here all night."

"Have you found out anything, Nate?"

"No. But I do want you to know that I think you are looking great, Rachel."

"You look pretty good yourself, Nate."

"In case anything happens to us, Rachel, I want to apologise for walking out on you four years ago."

"Forget it, it was for the best, Nate."

"No hard feelings?"

"No hard feelings!" Rachel answered. Nate put out his hand. Rachel shook it."

"Thanks. I didn't want to go to my grave without straightening that out."

"What's with this 'going to my grave' thing?"

"I've got a funny feeling, Rachel," Nate confessed. "Something is telling me I'm not going to get back."

"You're just as bad as Gran, Nate," Rachel complained. "Whatever happened to common sense?"

"There's a steamship coming into the harbor," Gran's words interrupted their conversation.

"It's the "Princess Beatrice," Gran continued, pointing out to sea. "She's a CPR steamer that used to steam up from Vancouver to Prince Rupert. I rode on her myself when I was a child. She must be here for the prisoners."

"Maybe we can at least get back to civilization," Nate commented. "Maybe if we go back to where we disappeared something might happen," he growled.

All four of them crowded into the small boat taking the prisoners out to the steamer. No one on the ship seemed to be able to see or hear them.

The day passed in frustration for Rachel. There were still a lot of unsaid things she wanted to discuss with Nate. She tried to find a spot to be alone but was forced to sit in the crowded passenger space with Gran and Nigel and the others as the "Beatrice" worked her way down the coast. The older couple's presence prevented Rachel from initiating any kind of frank discussion with Nate. By the end of the day Nigel had an entire pad filled with drawings.

"You're not going with them?" Nate protested as Gran, Nigel and Rachel started to follow the prisoners as they were herded into two ancient trucks, presumably to take them to Oakalla.

"Raven wants Rachel to witness and record what happens here," Gran said obstinately.

"Oh, my God," Nate commented.

"Gran's having hallucinations, Nate," she told him. "I have to stay and protect her."

Gran crowded into one of the trucks with the prisoners. There was no room left in the trucks so Rachel grabbed onto the back of one of them, next to a large Kwakiutl man who didn't fit in the truck, either. Nate pushed up against her and grabbed onto the latch on the back door. Nigel stood precariously on the bumper hanging on to Nate. The old truck lurched forward and all three of them grasped onto anything they could grab.

"Thank God we're not going very fast," Nigel said.

The native prisoner started shouting something loudly as we wove through the streets of Vancouver and then New Westminster on the way to Oakalla. It sounded like "hap, hap." The other prisoners in the truck cheered loudly.

"What's he shouting?" Rachel questioned Nate.

"He's probably just nuts," Nate answered.

"Remember Dear?" Gran shouted from inside the truck. That's the "Hamatsa" cry from the Winter Ceremonial dance of the Kwakiutl. "Don't you recognize it? "Hap, Hap," it means "Food, Food." You saw Bob Harris dancing it. That fellow next to you is Herbert Martin. He was one of the well known secret societies dancers the other night. Witness how he refuses to be intimidated by the orders of the white colonial government trying to extermi-nate our ancient culture."

Rachel stared at the prisoner next to her in awe. She realized that Gran was right, that he was trying to keep up the spirits of the others in the trucks. People on the streets stared at Herbert Martin in derision as he kept the "Hamatsa" cry up all through the passage to Oakalla. But he wasn't the slightest deterred.

"That's how our culture survived," Gran shouted. "Because of people like Herbert Martin."

It took forever to get to Oakalla. The trucks kept having flat tires. They were not used to carrying so many people. At the prison Rachel and Gran followed the ladies in through one door. The last she saw of Nate and Nigel, they were following some of the men in through another door.

Rachel could tell the four women from the Kwakiutl villages were completely terrified. She and Gran sat on one of the bare benches in the intake room as the women were forced to undress and were strip searched one by one by laughing male guards. They took the woman's fingerprints while they were still standing naked and shivering in fear. The guards looked over each of the woman and wrote down any irregularities (large head, weight irregularity, birthmarks) and the ladies measurements onto some kind of file records after reading them out loud. The four women were com-pletely mortified.

"You know how Kwakiutl people are about the privacy of their bodies, Rachel," Gran spoke. Her voice was full of outrage. "Those ladies had never been violated like that before."

"Look at the front of the old one's head," one of the guards laughed. "It's slanted."

"Do those guards have to enjoy their jobs so much?" Rachel complained to Gran.

"They undoubtedly have orders from Government officials to teach these Indian people a lesson this time, Dear," she replied. "To make an example of them to others and humiliate them so much that they will never dare to dance the Potlatch again or break any other restrictions of the Indian Act, particularly submitting their Indian Land Claim petitions to the Privy Council in England. But how little they know."

"What do you mean, Gran?"

"The treatment these people received was reported to all the coastal and interior tribes, Dear. These arrests did more to strengthen our resolve to hold onto our customs and pursue our land claims than anything else that happened since the white man invaded our territories. The culture went underground instead of people practising outright defiance. Land Claim activities switched to the Native Brotherhood in Alaska and went on underground. That's how the culture survived until now."

Rachel's thoughts returned to the ordeal the four Kwakiutl ladies were going through.

After being strip searched, their body measurements written down and commented on, and fingerprinting in the nude, the four ladies were issued ill fitting prison dresses. Then they were ordered to pick up rough, cotton mattress covers, fill them with unprocessed straw and move into small cells with bars on their windows. The cells had a foul-smelling odour that nauseated Rachel. She and Gran followed Florence Knox into her cell and sat down on the cold cement floor. Rachel retched, the place was so ghastly and smelly. She felt so sorry for the ladies. Florence Knox was sobbing uncontrollably and she could hear the others crying openly in their cells.

Gran and Rachel stayed with Florence Knox for the full ten days the ladies were locked up in the foul-smelling cells without so much as even an exercise break. A strange mixture of emotions whirled through Rachel's head. Anger at the government's treatment of the Potlatcher's was mixed with confusion over relationship issues. No one had come along to replace Nate after they had broke up. Rachel felt intense negativity. She reminded herself that she had made a vow to put a moratorium on relationship pressures at least until she finished her doctorate. She managed to acknowledge that she was presently afraid for her and Gran's present circumstances and that her sense of reality was being badly shaken. There was no way to make sense of the weird happenings.

The Kwakiutl ladies were thoroughly demoralized. Breakfast consisted of mush without milk or sugar, black coffee and half a piece of toast. Dinner was an bowl of very thin stew. It's contents were unrecognizable.

Rachel and Gran met up with Nate and Nigel again as all the prisoners were released into the courtyard to do some grounds cleaning after ten days.

Nate rushed over to Rachel.

"We need to have a talk, Rachel."

"I know," she replied.

Gran and Rachel learned that the men had been imprisoned for ten days in tiny cells without a break as well.

"It was awful," Rachel told Nate. "Do you know they strip searched these ladies. Florence Knox keeps having heart palpitations and the guards are just ignoring her complaints."

"That's nothing, Darling," Nigel replied. Rachel noticed he had even more sketch pads in his hands. "Do you know what they did to the men? The small ones were issued prison garb that were too big for them and the large ones were issued prison garb miles below their size. It was done deliberately to humiliate them, I'm sure. A fire hose was even turned on them at one point."

"Can you believe that they are deliberately sending the Chiefs of the villages to feed the pigs?" Nate asked. He sounded angry.

"You've changed, Nate?" Rachel commented. "I thought you didn't care what happened to Heiltsuk culture. Remember, all you cared about was becoming the first Heiltsuk man to become Superintendent of one of the big fish companies."

"I know, Rachel." Nate sounded apologetic. "I'm sorry, believe me. I've had all kinds of time to think since we've been in this prison."

"What made you come on this trip, Nate?"

Nate smiled ruefully. "My boss volunteered me. You know his wife, Clarissa. She's obsessed with successful conclusion of the Land

Claims. It's Clarissa that thought of this 'Voyage of Solidarity' to demonstrate First Nations Unity on the Land Claims situation."

"See that older lady," Gran interrupted. "She's the wife of a chief, Mary Whonnock. I guess the government made sure several of the chiefs were sentenced so they could be thoroughly humiliated."

"They made Florence Knox come down here even though her elderly husband is very ill," Rachel said, her mind going back to the plight of the ladies. She cried herself to sleep almost every night."

As Rachel spoke the voyageurs suddenly felt myself being thrown to the ground. The grounds of the prison suddenly started spinning.

"What's happening?" Rachel cried out. She felt her chest being crushed somehow by some kind of force-field again.

"Don't worry," Gran cried. "It's "Raven," returning us to the present."

"Rachel," Nate cried out. "Remember we need to have a talk." That was the last thing Rachel heard as she lost consciousness again.

When Rachel woke up she found myself lying inside a bobbing, dugout canoe in a raging sea. Someone's jacket had been thrown over her. She stared around trying to force her eyes to focus.

"Just stay still," one of the women paddlers advised. Rachel recognised her friend Rose Alfred from the Nuu'chah'nulth Nations' canoe.

"Don't try to move," Rose warned. "You're safe now, I think, that is if we can get this canoe to shore at Neah Bay before this wind gets any worse."

Rachel's vision cleared. She stared around her, desperately searching for Nate and Gran. She couldn't stop shivering. Her canoe mates were crammed together amongst tired-looking paddlers wearily stroking as they tried to pull their overcrowded dugout to the shore.

"Gran?" Rachel asked anxiously. "And Nate Archer? They're not in the canoe. And Nigel Kent?"

"Everyone except Nate Archer is safe," Rose told her. "A small yacht managed to pick your grandmother and Nigel Kent out of the water. We've picked up the others but no one knows what happened to Nate Archer."

"Nate's missing?" Rachel gasped. Rachel felt intense emotion flooding into her stomach and heart.

"We're not sure what happened. Several people swear a boat picked up Nate when he was near the shore. But if the boat picked him up it never dropped him off. No one's heard anything on the radio from them."

"There was a boat!" Rachel gasped. "I saw it myself."

"Maybe we'll hear something when we reach shore, Rachel. You just try and relax."

"Everyone else is safe?" she queried again.

"It's a miracle," Rose told her. "That only Nate Archer is missing. I was so scared when we saw your canoe overturn. It took us so long to get to you and that water must have been so cold. Thank God the wind blew your canoe back in our direction. Otherwise we would never have been able to reach you in time."

"Thank you," Rachel cried, tears filling her eyes. "All of you."

As the canoe reached shore people came running up.

"Where's Martha McBay," Rachel asked as someone helped her out of the canoe. "The older woman, she's the elder conducting the ceremonial chanting," she explained. "And have they found the missing paddler, yet."

"The older ladies's with one of my neighbours," one of the Makah Nation people of Neah Bay advised Rachel. "But the other fellow hasn't been located."

Sharp fear filled Rachel's stomach. Tears came into her eyes.

"There's wilderness around that shoreline where he might of landed. He might have got lost trying to go through the woods for help," the fellow tried to cheer Rachel up. "Don't worry, there's a search party out and boats are searching up and down the shore in case he's still in the water."

"Come on, I'll drive you to the older lady, myself," the man offered. Rachel's face was frozen with fear for Nate. The fellow helped her into one of the waiting cars near the beach.

"You're safe," she gasped as she entered the house of one of the Makah people and found Gran sitting on the chesterfield next to Nigel Kent, calmly drinking a hot cup of tea.

"Everyone is safe, Rachel, just like I told you."

Rachel staggered over to her side. Nigel looked at her in sympathy.

"Nate is missing, Gran," Rachel's voice had agony in it. "They're not sure if he reached shore. Some people think a boat picked him up but there's been no word from them."

"It might be connected to the death threats Rachel," Gran looked frightened and shocked. Suddenly her eyes looked funny.

"She's conferring with Raven, Rachel," Nigel Kent advised her.

"You believe that, Nigel?" Rachel gasped.

"Wait to you see what was in my pocket," Nigel warned. He sounded very odd. Rachel looked around the room to see if anyone was overhearing them. No one was present.

"Rachel, Raven doesn't know where Nate is," Gran explained. "But he thinks he's still alive and is in great danger."

"Sure, Gran." Rachel's heart froze at Gran's words.

"Rachel?" Nigel Kent queried.

She stared at him in shock.

"Rachel, I think we had better do what Martha wants us to do," he said. He pulled a pad of paper out of his pocket.

"What are you talking about, Nigel?"

"Martha says we two are to collaborate on a book about the history, Rachel. I believe her. Look at these."

Rachel stared at the pad in Nigel's hand. She froze.

"Nigel, those are the drawings you made at the Potlatch," she gasped. "And at the trial and prison. How did you bring them back?"

"I didn't, Rachel. I found them in my vest pocket when the fellow from the yacht pulled me into his boat."

Rachel stared at Nigel, not willing to believe him.

My clothes were soaked, Rachel," he explained. "But these drawings didn't have a drop of water on them."

"That's not funny, Nigel," Rachel told him. A shiver of fear ran down her spine.

"I'm not trying to be funny, Rachel. I'm only telling you what happened. There's no way these drawings should be dry. The water should have ruined them. Something supernatural must have protected them."

Rachel stared at Gran. Her eyes looked very intense. Somehow Rachel knew she had to take her seriously.

"I have to write a book, Gran?" she asked, her voice shaking with disbelief.

"And Nigel is going to illustrate it?"

"That's correct, Dear."

Rachel flipped through Nigel's pad. Her hands shook as she recognized the drawing of the Hamatsa that Nigel had made in the old school room at Alert Bay. She flipped through the others. They were drawings Nigel had done on the Princess Beatrice and at Oakalla Prison. She stared at him in disbelief.

"We had better not tell anyone about this, Darling," Nigel said. "They would throw us in for psychiatric assessment or something."

"That's where we should be, Nigel," Rachel gasped. "Undergoing psychiatric assessment."

"Trust me. Rachel," Gran said. "You're being given information about our people's past that the ordinary people of British Columbia need to know. Once they know the truth about the government treatment of our people they will be more willing to support the Land Claims. The history will be invaluable to you also when you try and understand and counsel some of our people. Information that your white university courses will never give you."

"If you say so Gran," Rachel's mind reeled. She realized that she was in the same boat as Nigel. Despite her graduate training she realised that she didn't have any rational explanation of the mystifying events that was any better than the explanation Gran had given. Rachel realised that her rational mind was thoroughly blown away by what had happened and Nate Archer's disappearance.

"I only hope we don't have to be thrown out of canoes into freezing water every time Raven wants us to learn something." Rachel muttered. "Particularly with Nate Archer missing."

"We would have been thrown out anyway, Rachel. Going on in that wind today was a big mistake. Raven was just taking advantage of the timing," Gran explained.

"Sure, Gran." Rachel realised she didn't have the strength to argue any more.

CHAPTER 4

Nigel Kent

It was just barely light as Nigel Kent moved onto the beach at Neah Bay where the canoes had been unexpectedly stranded for the last week. He had spent the night rolling and turning. Dreams about Martha McBay kept assailing him. He hoped for inspiration from the magnificent sunrise as it's brilliant orange and yellow hues filled the sky. He listened, hoping for intuitive answers, to the rhythmic sound of the waves as they rolled into the pebble-covered beach.

What astounded Nigel was that it wasn't just Nate Archer's disappearance and his mind-altering experiences back in time that was bothering him. It came as a shock to acknowledge it but Nigel realized that despite the trauma around him he was becoming thoroughly infatuated with Martha McBay. He admitted to himself that he found the older, First Nation's woman very attractive.

"And I thought I had come to terms at last with relationship issues," he mused. "I was determined to devote myself to my art, and now look what's happened."

"And Martha would never consider me a romantic interest for one moment," he mused. "The way she feels about the way white governments have treated her people. Perhaps if I could please her somehow. Maybe if I do a superb job with the illustrations for Rachel's book it will impress Martha?"

"Hi, Nigel," Rachel disturbed his thoughts.

"Good morning, Darling," Nigel gave Martha's beautiful grand-daughter a warm greeting. Nigel realized that Rachel and the other paddlers were just as depressed and frightened as he was at the failure to locate Nate Archer.

"We'll just have to presume that Martha is right, Rachel, that Nate Archer is still alive."

"I can't think straight, anymore, Nigel. Do you really suppose it's possible that Gran might be giving us messages from some source of Native spirituality?"

"Why not, Rachel? I've come into contact with many indigenous people in my travels around the world. I've known many of them to be extremely spiritual even if their experiences don't fit into the framework of academic Psychology, like you've studied. Your grandmother is a very special lady, believe me!"

Nigel didn't realise it but his tone of voice was betraying his regard for Martha.

"You think a lot of Gran, don't you, Nigel?"

Nigel's face went beet red. He realised he had lost objectivity about Martha McBay and that he was revealing the depth of his emotions to her grand-daughter.

"Yes, My Dear," he confessed. "Now, since you've detected my interest in your grandmother, tell me, do you suppose Martha would ever allow herself to be courted by a Caucasian? Particularly one that comes from England?"

"Nigel!" Rachel looked at him with considerable concern. "Gran is in her seventies, although she doesn't look anywhere near it. People always think she's much younger. But frankly, isn't she a little old for you?"

"All my relationships have been with women older than me, Rachel," he explained.

Nigel neglected to tell Rachel that for some reason he was always attracted to mature ladies. Ones that seemed to possess unusual knowledge. Ladies that exuded spirituality, higher learning, maturity way beyond the norms.

"I am in my late sixties, myself, now, you know."

"I thought you were much younger, Nigel," Rachel looked quite startled. "How many relationships have you had, anyway?"

"Quite a few, My Dear," he confessed. "Although I must admit that some of them were rather brief. Quite intense but brief."

"I don't know about Gran, Nigel. "You're right, she doesn't have very good opinions about Caucasian people. But there are some she admires. Like Shirley MacLaine, for instance."

"Shirley MacLaine? Really. Maybe there is a chance? Whatever does Martha admire about Shirley MacLaine?"

"Her courage to endure ridicule for her beliefs. And her free thinking. Gran's always admired those qualities in anyone."

Nigel felt his hopes raise.

"You won't mention this conversation to Martha, will you?"

"No, of course not, Nigel."

Nigel decided to change the topic. "I'll find a way into Martha's heart, somehow," he vowed to myself.

"It's a good thing the managing committee's decided not to delay us any longer, Rachel. Clarissa says that a show of solidarity is vital for the continuance of the land claims. She says that members of both governments are beginning to waffle. Despite our mishap, the death threats and Nate Archer's disappearance, I don't think we have any choice but to go on. Any more delay and we wouldn't have a hope of reaching Bella Bella by the gathering date. We might just be able to make the date if we give it all we have."

"They're sending a new Dugout Coordinator, Nigel?"

"Yes. Do you know Nate's cousin Paul Archer? Clarissa sent him down until we get the Nate Archer situation resolved."

"Oh, no! Paul Archer is a radical activist, Nigel. Or so Nate told me. I've never met him but Nate told me he was pretty far out for an 'Archer.' I think he was even arrested. At the blockages of railroad expansion in the Gitskan confrontation."

"That's why Clarissa is sending him down, Rachel. She figures we might need someone familiar with terror tactics to deal with whoever is responsible for Nate's disappearance."

"My God, I wonder what he looks like? Like a Counter-Culture person out of the sixties, I suppose, or one of those far out environmental activists." Nigel chuckled. "Not your usual psy-

chologist-type, I guess, Rachel. Anyway, you'll find out soon
enough. If I'm not mistaken, that's him, coming towards us now."
    Anxiety filled Nigel's thoughts as he stared at the man coming
towards them on the beach. It had been over a week since Nate
Archer had disappeared and no trace of him had been found. Nigel
suspected that, as odd as it sounded, what Martha McBay had
said about the matter was correct. That Nate was alive but in great
danger. And God only knew where he might be.
    "I've got to stop thinking about Nate," he told himself. "My
job is to get the documentary about this voyage together. And I
need to help Paul Archer get the canoes moving again."
    Clarissa's directions on the phone came back to him.
    "I'm sending you a new Dugout Coordinator, Nigel. He's a
strong person, an activist connected to the American Indian Movement. You know how important this voyage is to the First Nations
people of B. C. that have submitted land claims to the Treaty
Commission. We're all depending on the canoes coming into the
mouth of the harbor exactly on the time the Commencement exercises start. I hope you'll help Paul Archer accomplish that goal."
    "Of course, My Dear," Nigel had assured her.
    "Hi, you must be Nigel Kent." Nigel smiled as he noticed
Rachel's intense inspection of Paul Archer. He could tell the fellow
wasn't at all like she had expected.
    "She was expecting some motorcycle type wearing a leather
jacket, I guess," he thought. "And here's this handsome fellow
looking every bit an intellectual, if you ask me."
    Paul Archer did have long hair. But it was professionally styled
and fit in with his rather fashionable "Fila" track suit.
    "And you must be Rachel McBay," Paul Archer said, a warm
smile lighting up his attractive facial features, and his voice exud-
ing charm. "You're every bit as lovely as I remember Nate telling
me."
    "Pleased to meet you," Rachel managed. A slight flush to her
face betrayed the powerful first impression Paul Archer was making on her.

A group of paddlers appeared on the scene. Nigel realised that Martha McBay had arrived to do the opening spiritual exercises that were practised every morning on the beach before the canoes left.

"You know Martha McBay," I presume.

"Indeed I do," Paul answered. He gave Rachel's grandmother a warm hug.

"Glad to have you with us, Dear."

The paddlers formed their customary circle on the sand. Nigel could feel his own fears about the death threats and Nate Archer's disappearance reflected in the paddlers all around him.

Martha chanted her customary chants with Rose Alfred drumming for her. Then she changed to English.

"It's important today for all of us to release any negativity and disharmony before we embark on today's voyage," she instructed. "We need to ask the 'ancestors' today for an influx of power, the power of strength and commitment for each other that we will need to successfully complete this journey."

Nigel smiled in admiration as he realised that Martha was trying to give all the paddlers the courage to overcome their fears and doubts.

"Martha's right," Paul Archer joined in. "We must make the effort to become part of something bigger than ourselves," he added. "So that we can release the creativity that will allow us to be successful on this journey. That is all that is asked of us. We acknowledge that as 'two leggeds' we are not perfect, but we ask for guidance. Let us strive to attain greater awareness of all that is and try to live up to the Indian spiritual principle of love for all life."

"He's not what I expected," Rachel found herself extremely interested in Paul Archer. "He sounds just like Gran."

Nigel could tell that the new Dugout Coordinator was making a great impression on all the paddlers.

Martha returned to the chants and the songs that she used every morning that enabled the paddlers to lose any anger, resentment, fear or self-doubting they might be experiencing. Nigel could feel a great cloud of dark energy leaving them as the two groups of paddlers set out again on the journey they had failed to accomplish a week earlier.

"We've got to get this dugout one half of the way to Port Angeles by nightfall," Paul Archer directed.

"Shouldn't we make sure the canoes are always together?" Rachel suggested. Her voice sounded anxious.

"Yes, Rachel," Paul agreed. "Believe me our canoes are never going to get separated again."

"New safety regulations," Paul explained.

"Look at the Eagle," Rose Alfred from the Nuu'chah'nulth canoe shouted as the two canoes moved in unison out of the beach at Neah Bay. Nigel looked up. A huge, golden eagle had come down from the hills behind the beach and was heading straight for the canoes. The eagle circled over them twice and then headed straight for the bend in the coast that would lead the canoes into Cape Flattery.

"It's an omen," Martha McBay decreed. "Eagle is showing us the way."

Both canoes moved off at a good pace towards Cape Flattery again.

Nate Archer's cousin was seated next to Rachel. Nigel took another good look at the fellow. He noted that Paul's long, black, shiny hair hung down to his shoulders and that Paul had the slightly fair skin of some Heiltsuks, along with his cousin Nate's good looks.

"Where did you get the new video camera, Nigel?" Martha asked as he took another camera out of a bag.

"I always have a spare, Darling," he answered. "Look right into the camera, now. That's it Dear, start the drumming and the chanting. That's the sequence I lost when we all landed in the water."

Martha started to drum rhythmically in the front to set the pace. Nigel nodded approvingly at her and the others' courage in returning so quickly after the death threats and Nate's disappearance. He noted with approval that Martha had abandoned the heavy ceremonial robes that had almost cost her life.

"Drum a little faster, Darling," he ordered. Nigel tried to ignore the effect she was having on his heart.

Martha speeded up the drumming. The others picked up their paddling pace and the canoes moved rapidly forward. By noon they had moved around Cape Flattery and towards the Strait of Juan De Fuca.

"Look at the dolphins," Paul Archer yelled in an excited voice. "White-sided, Spinner dolphins," he pointed ahead of the canoe.

"Look, they're leaping out of the water ahead of us," he added. Nigel shifted his video camera and refocused on the dolphins.

"Marvellous," he cried. Two white-sided, Spinner dolphins were leaping in and out of the ocean in advance of the canoes.

"It's another omen," Martha McBay decreed. "Look, they're leading the way for us. Listen carefully," she ordered everyone. "If you concentrate enough you might even hear voices from our ancestors. Sometimes, on voyages like this, one of your ancestors even gives you your song."

"Indeed?" Paul agreed.

"Or sometimes the ancestors give you a vision," Martha's voice informed the paddlers. "A vision of your path in life," she said.

Nigel wondered if his path in life included an intense encounter with Martha McBay. He acknowledged that she was one of the most fascinating women he had ever encountered.

One of the paddlers, Ernie Alfred, who had participated in the Qatuwas voyage in 1993, suddenly started wailing a chant in his native language. He was allowing himself to sing one of the songs he had received on the Qatuwas voyage.

Martha rhythmically matched her drumming to Ernie's chant. Nigel aimed the camera at Ernie, picking up his chant with the audio controls.

"It must be the power of suggestion," Rachel muttered to Paul. Her scientific training was taking another slam.

"Don't be too sure, Rachel," Paul Archer corrected her. "Subjective spiritual experiences don't need to be proven scientifically. They only need to be validated internally."

"That's not what my professors taught me," Rachel argued. "They class the type of experience like Ernie Alfred is having under para-psychology. They link them with psychic experiences and near-death testimonies. Psychologists explain these type of experiences as attempts by the brain to explain perceptual experiences during sleep or a light hypnotic state."

"You've studied Psychology, haven't you?" Paul Archer looked sympathetically at Rachel. "Clarissa told me that you're nearly through your Doctorate."

Rachel nodded.

"I'm a lawyer." Rachel went into shock. "But I don't let my legal training get into the way of my spiritual training."

"And you're an activist?" Rachel said, her voice betraying her opinion of activists.

"Indeed," Paul Archer laughed. "And a student of Native Spirituality. I really get angry when those stuff-shirt professors put down legitimate, subjective, spiritual experiences of First Nations' people."

"Like I just did? By saying that Ernie's song is just the power of suggestion."

"Exactly, Rachel. You're just echoing your ignorant professors' assumptions. As far as I'm concerned I don't think those fellows have the right to open their mouths as experts on anything except technical aspects of Psychology."

"Whatever do you mean, Paul?"

"By their very classification, Rachel. "Para- psychology. It means beyond Psychology. Exactly. Subjective spiritual experiences are beyond their methods of study. Psychologists have never studied First Nation's Spirituality with an open mind, or for that matter, anything that can't be measured and crunched into their numerical, statistical systems."

"That's pretty strong, Paul," Rachel felt like she did when she was arguing with her grandmother.

"Not any stronger than their condemnation of anything that

doesn't fit into the belief system of modern Psychology. You're familiar, I'm sure, with those "Sceptic Societies" those fellows set up. If you ask me. the belief system they cling to is as much a "consensus" agreement as anything else."

"That's what Gran tells me, Paul," Rachel complained. "According to her, I've been wasting my time studying in the white man's educational system. She thinks I should get more in touch with Native belief systems if I'm going to work amongst our people."

"That's good advice, Rachel, if you ask me."

Rachel fell silent. Somehow she found Paul's mental trysting with her invigorating as well as irritating.

The canoe paddlers were in for an endurance run. The canoe had to make it one half of the way to Port Angeles before darkness struck as Nigel didn't consider running lights to be traditional.

Fortunately there was no sign of the powerful winds of the other day. Just a medium chop on the water.

By the afternoon the voyage was becoming almost hypnotic. Ocean travel had calmed down, and the paddlers were becoming rather drowsy with the sound of paddles moving up and down, the breaking of the waves against the canoe and the rhythmic cries of sea gulls disturbing the peace of the open ocean. Even the hurried snack breaks with half of them eating their bagged lunches at the time seemed almost robotic.

By dusk the steady paddling was taking it's toll. Nigel looked at the paddlers and empathised with their weary expressions. He could feel his own arms protesting fiercely as he continued to film with the video camera. By the time the paddlers had located a suitable rest stop for the night the sun was barely above the water.

Paul Archer directed the paddlers of the two canoes to pull their dugouts above the high tide line for the night and unload their tents and provisions. Before long a roaring fire was burning on the shore. Rachel, Paul, Nigel, Martha and Rose Alfred from the Nuu'chah'nulth canoe sat down on one of the logs and ravenously ate their hastily prepared dinner.

CHAPTER 5

West Coast Vancouver Island Problems

"When did you learn to chant like you were doing today?" Rachel asked Rose Alfred as Nigel and Paul Archer went off to plan for the next day. Suddenly with Paul Archer around Rachel found she was interested in Native Spirituality. Rose's chants had been floating over the water all day.

"Very recently," Rose Alfred admitted.

"I'm envious," Rachel found herself confessing. With her new found interest, Rachel realised that she was also curious about the deep bond that was being formed amongst the paddlers as a result of the rituals and chanting that were taking place daily and during the paddling. "How did you learn to chant?"

"It hasn't been easy," Rose Alfred confided. "I'm from Nitinaht Lake, near Bamfield. "I learned to chant during the last few years. Healers have been present amongst our people trying to help with the sex abuse and low self-worth problems that had all but destroyed any hope of a normal life in our village."

"That's pretty heavy-duty."

"It's the same all over, Rachel," Martha McBay interrupted. "You've been away attending school. You don't realise the extent of the social problems in the coastal villages."

"What happened in your village?" Rachel queried Rose.

"Sex abuse," Rose answered. She went on to fill Rachel and Martha McBay in on what had happened on the remote and rugged west coast of Vancouver Island.

Rose Alfred told them about the several generations of her

relatives that were sent to either the Christie or Alberni Indian Residential Schools for ten months of the year and how they missed the normal socialization period in their villages during which the traditions and ways of the coastal natives were passed on to the young. On top of that, Rose recounted how many of the male students had experienced sexual molestation and abuse at the hands of a paedophile hired as the dormitory supervisor for over twenty years at the Alberni school.

Rose related how a generation gap had resulted when the students lost their native language because the school forced them to use only English and the elders only spoke the Native language. She recounted how massive unemployment occurred after 1945 when the fishing industry concentrated itself in the Cities, closing local canneries. Unemployment, despair, and alcohol abuse became the norm in the villages.

"To make it short, alcohol abuse and hidden sex predation was everywhere," Rose testified. "When I was thirteen I was molested and raped by the father of one of the families I was baby-sitting for. No one would believe me when I told them what had happened. That totally destroyed both my trust in those around me and my self-worth. Years later when I moved back to the reserve from a failed marriage in Vancouver, I confronted the individual who had abused me. I was afraid for my own young children."

"What happened?"

"At first it was awful," Rose testified. "I was threatened and myself and my children were called everything under the sun. But a native healer was called in and talking circles were formed. It took years but finally the cycle of victimisation is being broken in our village. Many have come forward, confessed their crimes, asked forgiveness and things have drastically improved for our children."

"That's amazing," Rachel said. "Ordinarily there's very little hope of changing sex predators using traditional methods. I know, I've researched the studies and they all say the same thing. Aversive therapy and Social Skills Training only go so far. It's the same for repeat criminals. The only positive thing the research talks about is that the longer a criminal remains in the system the less likely he is to repeat the crime."

"I told you the white educational system doesn't have the answers for Native people, Rachel," Martha McBay interjected.

Rose Alfred sensed the tension that her grandmother's words caused Rachel.

"Anyway, sorry to blabber on like that," she apologised. "But learning the old healing ways has been a lifesaver for me. And for our village. That's how I found my songs, and learned to chant. It really turned my oldest son, Jerry's, life around, too." "I really appreciate you sharing this with us, Rose," Rachel told her. "What helped Jerry?"

"Helping building the Nuu'chah'nulth dugout canoe, Rachel. For this voyage. Jerry hasn't touched the alcohol he was becoming addicted to since he joined in with the Canoe Society that built our canoe. And you know he's paddling up to Bella Bella with us. I haven't been this happy for a long time, believe me. Now, if we could only find out what happened to Nate Archer."

The trio went off for bed for the night.

The next day the canoes made it to Port Angeles without any problems. Rachel felt tears in her eyes as the black canoe of the Squamish Nation with the elaborate white and red designs at the front rendezvoused with the Heiltsuk and Nuu'chah'nulth canoes exactly on time.

The next morning after the cleansing rituals all three canoes travelled across the busy Strait of Juan De Fuca without incident. Rachel felt her whole body strengthening remarkably through the constant exertion caused by the steady paddling.

"Do you see them?" Gran asked the paddlers in the middle of the strait."

"See who, Gran?" Rachel wondered if her grandmother was having hallucinations again.

"The Ancestors, Dear. They're all around us. In spirit canoes. They're helping us get safely through this busy shipping passage."

Rachel looked at the tears in several of the paddlers' eyes, and the emotions on their faces. Ernie Alfred and several other of the paddlers that had been in the Qatuwas journey in 1993 were nodding their heads affirmatively to Gran's question. Rachel noticed Paul Archer giving her a look. She stopped herself from blurting out any verbal invalidation of Gran's and the paddler's experiences this time. Somehow Paul Archer's opinion of her mattered.

"Very good, Rachel," Paul Archer gave her a warm smile. All Rachel could think of was how attractive he was.

"I've been studying too long," she thought. "There must be more to life," she decided, throwing her moratorium on relationships out the window.

"There it is," Ernie Alfred cried later, pointing to a thin line of smoke drifting vertically into the air as the sun was almost disappearing into the ocean below the horizon. "The signal fire from the Sooke nation."

"Head for that fire," Paul ordered.

As our two canoes neared the shore Martha McBay called out an ancient greeting chant asking permission to come into the Sooke Nation land. An answering chant floated out over the water.

"Go for it," Paul Archer ordered. The paddlers intensified their efforts and within several minutes the canoes were safely up on the beach. The welcoming members of the Sooke tribe hugged the paddlers from both the canoes warmly. The Sooke Nation canoe was on the beach ready to join the voyage.

Rachel stared at the front of the Sooke Nation canoe as the light dimmed.

"See the protrusion carved into the bow, below the ears of the carved wolf head, Rachel?" Paul Archer asked. Rachel nodded. "And those painted eyes? Those are the "heart" of the canoe. So it can sense and be aware of where it's going."

"You think canoes have some kind of consciousness, Paul?"

"Of course they do, Rachel. The spirit of the great cedar they are cut from is still with them."

"At least he must think I can be educated," Rachel sighed.

Rachel and Gran joined the paddlers and the Sooke Nation

people as they started to take part in a "Pow Wow" around a huge fire that had been built on the shore. After some ceremonial speeches the paddlers were shown sleeping spaces for the night and led to a food tent.

"Thank God we're making such good time, " Nigel thought as he wearily went to sleep for the night.

The four canoes arrived at Victoria, the Capital of British Columbia the next day.

"Clarissa will be pleased," Nigel realised. "We've already made up one of the lost seven days."

The canoes slowed as Martha McBay chanted the request for entry onto Songhees land. An answering chat echoed out over the waters and the paddlers went ashore.

Hundreds of well-wishers from the Songhees Nation were lined up on the beach and the paddlers were ceremoniously conducted into cars and driven to a huge longhouse in Victoria.

"That's Eagle and Bear Mother," Martha McBay told Rachel, pointing to the totem outside the longhouse.

Inside the log and cedar plank structure it was evident that a veritable potlatch awaited their presence. Food and drinks were brought immediately and the paddlers lost some of their weariness from crossing the Strait of Juan De Fuca. Paul waved off any alcohol for the group as one of the rules for the journey was that all paddlers would remain alcohol free. Nigel sat down alongside Martha McBay and gave her a warm smile.

The Potlatch started immediately. Singers dressed in ceremonial robes came out from behind the wings and started chanting.

"Do you realised that the Potlatch was only revived in Victoria in 1994?" Paul Archer asked Rachel. "Really?" she answered.

"That's Salishan, the language of the Coast Salish, Martha McBay informed them.

"They are singing songs of honor for the dead."

Rachel realised she was getting a double dose of education. To Nigel the chants sounded eerily familiar to the ones he had heard on Village Island before. Nigel had brought along his video camera and he was contentedly filming all the happenings. After the chantors left a number of male dancers leaped aggressively out onto the stage.

"What kind of mask is that, Martha?" Nigel asked. One of the dancers was wearing a mask very different from the ones he had viewed the other time.

"It's the Skhway-Khwey mask of the Coast Salish secret dance societies, Nigel," she answered. "This is the Spirit Dance."

"What is the "Spirit Dance" about Martha?"

"It's about communication, Dear, between the living and those that have gone on before."

"I feel like I'm at a seance," Rachel told Paul Archer, forgetting to censure her comments.

"You need to give your grandmother more credit, Rachel," Paul corrected. He gave Rachel direct eye contact for a long time.

"Why does that look do something to me?" Rachel thought.

"Believe me, I've been to a number of these Spirit Dances. And to Ghost Dances and Sun Dances all over Canada and the U. S. I've seen people completely transformed by these ceremonials."

Rachel felt like a small kid that had been censured.

Nigel focused his camera on the Coast Salish Skhway-Khwey mask. It was a large mask covering the head and shoulders of the dancer. In it's center and protuding several inches from the background were ornate, carved eyes and a nose. Eagle feathers rose high into the air above the face piece and abstract designs decorated the bottom below the mask.

"What do the feathers and the designs on that mask represent?" Nigel asked Martha McBay.

"That mask is rich in symbolism and Indian spiritual representations, Dear," Martha replied.

"If only I knew something about aboriginal culture," Nigel thought.

"Not being a Coast Salish," Martha continued, "I'm not exactly sure what they stand for, but I imagine some of those symbols represent important aspects of Native spirituality."

Dances continued for a couple of hours. Paul realised his paddlers had to be up at dawn.

"How are we going to get to Bella Bella on time if we have to attend all these celebrations on the way up?" he thought anxiously. Fortunately, the customary gift giving and name giving didn't last too long after that. The Songhees Nation dugout canoe that would accompany the others to Chemainus, their next stop, was blessed with eagle down and cedar broughs by a ritualist and the ceremonies ended. After conferring with the leaders of all the dugouts for navigational directions, Paul and Nigel accepted a ride back to the beach. They staggered wearily towards the tents that had been set up on the beach for the night.

As Paul and Nigel approached the tent they had been assigned to for the night they realised some one of the paddlers were sitting by themselves on some logs by a campfire that was still burning brightly. Nigel moved closer.

"That's Rachel and Martha," he said. He went over with Paul to encourage them to get a good sleep for the night.

Nigel sat down by Rachel. He sensed she was having a heavy-duty growth period.

"Don't worry, Darling," he reassured her. "It will all make sense, someday," he promised.

All of a sudden, just as Rachel got up to retire, the sand started to swirl. Everything started to revolve.

"What's happening, Martha?" Nigel demanded.

"Raven is giving us another history lesson, Dear."

"No!" Rachel protested to no avail. The force of the time vortex quickly knocked her unconscious.

CHAPTER 6

Indian Residential School Syndrome

"Where's Gran," Rachel thought as she tried to stop the gagging and retching she was experiencing. She realised she was regaining consciousness from what she was afraid was another time-travel experience.

Rachel looked around as her eyes focused and became aware of staring up at what looked like myriads of bed legs. She pulled herself to her feet despite the numbness in her limbs. Rachel gasped as she could see she was in a huge dormitory absolutely jammed with metal cots. The cots were all the same. Each cot had sheets, one blanket and a pillow at the top.

"Oh, God," she gasped, "we are back in the past again. I wonder if we'll find Nate Archer here?"

She glanced at the windows hoping they could be opened. There was a balcony outside and she could see stairs. Unfortunately she discovered that the windows had been nailed shut as she tried to open them.

Her eyes desperately searched for a way out. She spotted a Fire Escape sign but when she went to the door she realised it needed a key to open it. Feelings of being trapped descended on her and she rushed towards what she thought was another exit door as her eyes spotted it.

She pushed desperately against the door. It refused to open.

"Damn, it's locked," she said to herself as the door knob refused to move. Rachel panicked.

"Let me out," she pounded on the solid-looking door. "Let me out," she yelled. Suddenly the door opened. She gasped as Gran was standing outside, holding a huge dungeon key in her hand. "Calm down, Dear," Gran said, frowning slightly at Rachel. "It took me awhile to locate this key. I had to grab it off the sister who's the Dormitory Supervisor. Somehow I knew you were up here."

"Where are we Gran?" Rachel choked.

"Why, we're in in one of the Indian Residential Schools near Vancouver, B.C., around September 5th, nineteen forty-eight, if that newspaper on the table downstairs is right. Raven wants you to take a look at the cause of what your clinical psychologists label the 'Indian Residential School Syndrome,' if I'm not mistaken."

"Gran, I just want to get out of here," she protested. "We need to find Nate. Is he downstairs?"

"Nate is nowhere in sight, Dear, I'm afraid."

"Let's get out of here and look for him, Gran?"

"No, Dear, that's not why Raven's sent us here. Just concentrate on what you need to witness here. This Institution, and others like it all over Canada were the ultimate, white government solution to the Indian problem. If they could take the Indian out of us, using these schools, and assimilate us into white society it wouldn't cost them anything more in health, education costs or the land claims that our people stubbornly refused to give up. Besides, Paul Archer is here, too. We can't leave him alone to witness this by himself."

"Paul Archer," Rachel gasped in disbelief. "Paul Archer, our opinionated Dugout Canoe Coordinator?"

"It's you that are opinionated, Dear, if you ask me. Personally I find Paul Archer quite charming. I guess Raven wants him to view this school for some reason. And Nigel is here again too?"

Rachel's heart started pounding fiercely.

"Where are they, Gran?" she gasped. The intense look in her grandmother's eyes frightened her.

"They're downstairs, Rachel, watching a new batch of young girls going through their first day in this school. Just let me take a look at this dormitory. I went to a school myself like this, myself, once, Rachel, you know," Gran said. "But at an earlier time of course, back in the late nineteen twenties."

"See those cots. All of us had to sleep on cots like that on our right sides, with our hands in a prayer position under the pillows. Someone would check throughout the night and if you were in the wrong position you were shaken awake only to be spanked."

"And if you wet your bed during the night. The Dormitory Supervisor forced you to stand with the wet sheets over your head in the morning and apologize to the whole dormitory. If you were a repeat offender then you got whipped and you were forced to wash the sheets during breakfast time. You went without food." Gran's voice was full of emotion.

"I can't believe these institutions all look so much the same," she continued. "And time doesn't seem to make any difference. This dormitory looks almost like mine did, with beds next to each other and only room for a supervisor to move through looking for wrongdoing. But my dormitory was in the Alberni Residential School on Vancouver Island."

"Whatever were you doing in an Alberni school, Gran? Didn't you always live in Bella Bella, like you told me. Why didn't they send you to Fort Simpson. It was just up the coast."

"The white government and the churches that ran these schools wanted their pupils as far away as possible from their families, Dear. That way, the Indian children could be separated from their loved ones. Their culture, and their Indian spirituality could be taken away from them and their tribal customs and families could be discredited. For at least ten months of the year and sometimes for years. How better to make Indian children turn on their heritage and adopt the white values. Indoctrination is easier when there is no one around to counteract it."

"Gran, why are the windows all nailed shut here? Even the fire escape door is locked."

"So the student's don't run away, Dear. You don't think they would stay here if they had any choice, do you? Look at that fence outside, around those two separate playgrounds. See how it's got barb wire around the top to make sure students don't get out."

"Why do they have two playgrounds, Gran."

"One for the girls and one for the boys, Dear. In Indian Residential schools girls were not allowed to talk to boys, not even their brothers. All contact with the opposite sex was forbidden."

"Why, Gran?"

"Thoughts of the opposite sex were sinful, Rachel, to the clergy that ran Indian Residential schools."

"You never told me anything about your schooling, Gran?"

"I've never brought myself to say anything about that time, Dear or the Alberni Indian Residential School. Maybe that's why Raven's brought me here with you."

Gran looked uncomfortable as they walked down the huge, polished wooden staircase from the dormitory.

"I used to have to polish a staircase like this one, Dear," she confided in a shaky voice.

Rachel tried to listen to Gran despite her anxiety. She could tell Gran was bringing up upsetting, repressed memories from long ago.

"By hand, on my knees, for punishment, using my toothbrush to remove grime, everytime I was caught speaking our language," Gran continued. "And I had to polish the dining room furniture in the staff dining lounge. That was one of my chores I had to do every day. The Principal expected the staff's areas of the school to sparkle," Gran confided in a strange voice. "No dust was allowed, or," her voice cracked.

"Or, Gran?"

"You would do it again, Dear, because we were the lazy, dirty, little savages our Dormitory Supervisor told us we were, over and over again. She would wear white gloves when she checked our housekeeping chores. She'd run her hands over door sills and window ledges and if she picked up any dust anywhere then all of us had to spend our free time doing everything all over again."

"Gran, you were brought up a Methodist like most Heiltsuks,

Rachel stated. "The Alberni school was Presbyterian. How come you were sent to a Presbyterian Residential school miles away?"

"It didn't seem to matter to the Indian Agent that assigned you to the schools, Rachel. In B.C. religious denominations of all types vied for funds to set up residential schools. The Anglicans, Baptists, Presbyterians, United Church, Methodists and Roman Catholics ran day schools all over British Columbia before the white government decided to go residential. Even the Salvation Army got into the act."

Gran and Rachel located Paul Archer and Nigel as they reached the bottom of the staircase.

"What's going on Rachel?" Paul looked intense.

"We're back in the past, Paul. This happened before."

"How's this for a subjective experience that can't be scientifically validated, Rachel?"

"On a scale of one to ten this has to be a ten plus," she replied.

"You experienced being back in the past, Rachel and you don't believe in spirit communication at Spirit Dances? Boy, those establishment psychologists must have done a number on you."

"I would have thought you would be more questioning of Gran's superstitious explanations, yourself, Paul," Rachel found herself arguing with Nate's outspoken cousin. "After all you attended university, too?"

"I'm a practicing, Native activist. I've seen too many things during Native Spiritual ceremonies to accept any explanation some scientific type with a closed mind is going to give me. Particularly one who has been part of an establishment system that has been oppressing my people for over one hundred years."

"Gran says it's because of Raven, you know, the trickster God that the Haida and Heiltsuk people revere that we're being sent back into the past. That Raven's showing Nigel and I the history of what happened to our people. Gran wants me to write a book about the history and Nigel to illustrate it. What do you think?"

"I think your grandmother's explanation is a reasonable one, Rachel." Rachel could feel her scientific belief system weakening.

"You mean you were all in the past before. And Nate didn't

come back?"

"I don't know if Nate made it back from the past or not. Some paddlers swear they saw him being picked up by a boat. I'm sure I saw the boat going to him myself. Gran thinks he did make it back but she doesn't know where he is now. I know it doesn't make any sense Paul. But there doesn't seem to be anything that any of us can do to stop this."

"You and the others except Nate got back to the present again, Rachel."

"Yes, and now it appears we're being moved back and forth like ping-pong balls," she complained.

"Well, at least then, there's a good chance we won't be stuck here, forever."

"Pay attention to the the intake procedures," Gran interrupted. "Raven wants you to record this, Dear."

Rachel realised Nigel was on the steps staring at the new students.

"Better do as she says, Rachel," Nigel ordered. "It might be the only way to get ourselves back to the present."

Rachel tried to keep her mind on task. She looked down below. The large hallway of the school looked like a processing line in a factory. At the doorway, young girls were tearfully surrendering their clothes from home. Once they were down to their underwear, they moved on to a black-robed sister dispensing shoes and institutional clothing.

"I had to wear dresses like that," Gran said. "The wool was so scratchy. I used to develop hives all the time."

Paul had a look of total fascination on his face.

"What an opportunity," he muttered. "Now I'll be able to validate for myself the truth of some of the horror stories survivors are telling now about what happened to them in Residential Schools."

Paul's got nerves of steel, Rachel acknowledged. All this is doing for me is plunging me closer to a nervous breakdown.

She cringed suddenly as a small child further down the hall

started screaming below them.

A young girl who couldn't have been more than five and a half, was holding her face as a tall, nun, dressed in long black robes glared at her. The nun pulled the child's hand away from her face revealing a large red mark. Rachel realised that the cranky, older nun must have hit the child.

"Mother Jesus," Nigel muttured. "I've never seen anything so photogenic. Those black robes and that white cowl look so threatening as that nun looms over that child. And not a camera in sight. If only I could do a zoom as she towers over the child."

"Try a pad and pencil, again, Nigel." Rachel pointed at a desk near the front door.

"Thanks, Darling," Nigel made his way down to the desk. The pad disappeared from the front of it. Nigel came back and started to furiously draw the nun.

"That's the Mother Superior," Gran said.

"I warned you to not speak in your pagan Indian tongue," Mother Superior growled. "We speak only English in here." The little girl sobbed pitifully. Paul rushed over. He tried to put his arms around her and say something to her but the little girl obviously couldn't see, feel, or hear him.

"Inspect this one's hair again," Mother Superior ordered one of her subordinates. The nun's face was barely visible under her stark white cowl. A bunch of keys dangled menacingly from a leather strap on her robe. Another sister seized the child by the arm.

"That's the Dormitory Supervisor," Gran commented. Rachel watched as Gran slipped the upstairs key back onto her chain.

The nun shook the little girl when she tried to get out of her grasp. She ran her fingers through the girl's hair.

"No lice or nits," she said loudly. The other children looked at each other in horror.

"Spray her anyway," ordered Mother Superior. The nun sprayed from a bottle. Some foul-smelling stuff went into what little remained of the little girl's hair."

"What are they using?"

"DDT and kerosene is what they used when I was brought into my school," Gran replied.

"And get her to stop that infernal howling. I can tell she's going to be a troublemaker." Mother Superior stalked off and went into an office down the hall. The little girl cried again as the dormitory supervisor stuck her head in the huge tub of hot water that was on a raised platform in the middle of the hall. The dormitory supervisor plunged her head under the water several times until the child had the good sense to muffle her sobs.

"Get her out of Mother Superior's hearing range," the Dormitory Supervisor turned the little girl over to one of the older students who tried to comfort her. The student dragged the girl into one of the side rooms where students were emerging shorn of their braids and long hair. The Dormitory Supervisor moved to a small table near a line-up of new students who looked like their clothing issue was complete. Their short haircuts and ill-fitting new dresses made them all look alike.

"You are number 132," she said to a startled pupil at the head of the line as she stamped the number onto the girl's wrist with a large rubber stamp. "Take those clothes into the second room to the left down the hall," she ordered. "One of our older students will embroider your number onto all your clothes." "Remember. you are responsible for every one of these items. If any item becomes damaged or lost you will be punished severely."

The new student went down the hall carrying her worldly possessions, one spare dress, a spare pair of socks and underpants, a grey flanelette gown, a pair of heavy, black shoes, a bunch of hankerchiefs, and a coat that looked like it had been donated from a charity.

"The hankerchiefs were the worst," Gran said. "Every morning there was a hankerchief count and if you were missing even one of the seven they issued at the start of the school year you were shamed and punished."

"What's the grey flanelette gown for, Gran?" Rachel asked.

"That's to wear in the shower, Dear. In the Alberni Indian Residential School I had to wear one like that. I understand the boys all wore a type of plastic pants when they showered. When we were older and our breasts started to show we had to wear tight binders under our dresses at all times. Everything about the body was sinful."

The Dormitory Supervisor moved the stamp to the next number. Another student moved forward to receive her number.

"You are number 133," the sister said icily.

"Those numbers," Gran commented. "Quite often that was all anybody addressed you by. After awhile that's all you thought you were, some despised number from Hell. I've never forgotten mine. I was number 723," Gran told us.

"It was the underpants and the socks that caused the most embarrassment," Gran continued. "They had to be washed every night by hand and in the morning when they inspected, if there were any stains left on them you were punished severely."

"Welcome to Indian Residential School," Paul said, shaking his head in wonderment.

"Shut up your trap," the Dormitory Supervisor ordered one of the remaining girls who started to sob loudly. "I don't care if your shoes do pinch, you'll have Mother Superior disciplining all of us if you don't stop your howling and disturbing her mid-morning prayers. You'll just have to wear these."

"I have corns on my feet to this day from shoes like that," Gran commented. "And I was pigeon-toed when I entered the school. The nuns were determined to make me walk like the others. I had to force myself to walk at all times with my toes pointing outward. Otherwise I was put out in front of everyone and ridiculed."

As the students worked their way down the hall to have their belongings embroidered, the four time voyageurs went into one of the classrooms. Several rows of metal desks were lined up in the room with boys sitting in them. From the pictures on the walls they realised they were in some kind of religious instruction classroom. There were pictures of Hellfire and brimstone everywhere.

"I see some of you have forgotten how to sit over the summer," the tall nun who was instructing the boys complained. "Remember, it is expected that your backs will be straight as a rod and you will concentrate on my words at all times. Otherwise we can extend this lesson into your lunch time. You will recall that anyone who is late gets no food. Anyone who talks will be expected to kneel on the floor and hold their hands on top of their heads until lunch is over."

The few students that were slouching joined the others immediately in sitting firmly at attention.

"Antoine, explain our pictorial catechism on the wall to the new boys," the nun ordered.

"That's the roads to Heaven and Hell," Antoine stammered. The paddlers glanced closely at the colored print taking up most of the back wall. The road to Heaven was filled with people moving past angels and pastoral scenes to pearly gates with someone looking like St. Peter standing in front. The pilgrims on the road to Heaven were all white people. Nigel flipped his pad to a new page and feverishly copied the pictorial catechism.

The road to Hell was filled with people moving amongst devils and Satan's helpers until they arrived at a place with a huge firepit. The pilgrims on the road to Hell were all Indian people.

"And?" the nun demanded more from Antoine.

"I don't remember," Antoine stammered. A wooden pointer came out of the sister's robes and struck Antoine sharply on the knuckles of his right hand as it lay as instructed on the desk. Antoine flinced but didn't cry out.

"That's how we maintained dignity in these schools," Gran commented. "By silence. You defeated them if they couldn't make you cry."

"So you can't remember anything," the nun explained in a sarcastic tone. "Just like so many of you dumb Indians, it seems."

"The people on the left road are going to Heaven because they follow the rules of Jesus," the nun informed the class. "They make full use of their lands and resources, through agriculture and technology. The people on the right are going to Hell because they are pagan savages like you. They don't deserve to own land because they are too lazy to use it productively. They will always be beggars and paupers."

The students shifted uncomfortably in their seats.

"You can see what they taught in these schools," Paul whispered to Rachel. "Colonizing, Christianizing, racist attitudes, elitism and shaming."

A bell rang. The nun raised her pointer and looked for anyone daft enough to try to leave before she gave permission.

"You are expected to report to the dining room now, boys and the woodworking instructor at the shop behind the school immediately after lunch at 1:00. Remember, remain in line one after the other in the halls, no talking and absolutely no fraternizing with the girls if they happen to be in the same area of the school as you. Any food or drink items found being consumed on school property will be confiscated. From four to six you will do your assigned chores with the farm animals in the barns."

"Dinner will be exactly at six. It is expected that you will not leave any food on your plate, no seconds will be provided and evening service will start promptly at seven. Lights out are at nine and you will have showered, brushed your teeth, completed washing of your socks and underpants by that time, understood?"

"Remember the vow of silence in the morning when you dress and line up for Mass. Your homework from this class, due tomorrow, is to contemplate the following lesson:" the nun ordered, 'Denial of human comforts is a commitment to God.' I shall expect two pages of written work for tomorrow's class demonstrating this lesson."

"What a happy place!" Paul commented.

By the time the students had been taken to their beds that night the paddlers Rachel had seen enough to believe what Gran had been telling her all along. That she would not be able to sympathize completely with the damaged men and women of her people on the west coast unless she thoroughly understood what had happened to several generations of them in the Indian Residential School system. Rachel could no longer deny that that her people had undergone physical, emotional, and psychological abuse, not to mention miseducation and indoctrination in the Residential schools of her province. She was completely shaken.

"It was the loneliness that was the worst," Gran testified. "Except for a few whispered words under blankets at night we couldn't talk to each other in the only language we knew. We were trained never to even look at each other let alone a member of the opposite sex. We were trained to distance our emotions, never to complain, to obey orders without question and to parrot back whatever our teachers told us without question. We were trained to humiliate and shame each other."

"What happened after the students graduated from these schools, Martha?" Nigel asked. "Didn't they teach anything of value?"

"In my time, students mainly went back home to the reservations, Nigel, particularly the girls. We were not taught anything that would be valuable for finding work in the white man's society, only the cooking, cleaning, and sewing work that kept the Institution's running. The boys were taught agriculture and took care of the Institution's gardens, farm animals, building maintenance and grounds, but little good agricultural land was left to us on reserves. We were lucky if we knew how to read and write."

"Gran, did the same thing happen to our cousins on the Queen Charlottes?" Rachel asked. "What about the Haida people that come from there? What were they taught?"

"I'm from the Queen Charlottes, Rachel," Paul answered. "My ancestors were mainly sent to Edmonton, where they were forced to plough the lands on the Edmonton Indian Residential School by hand. For some reason the white government thought the future of the Queen Charlottes lay in agriculture."

"That's crazy, Paul." Rachel's mind reeled.

"I know," he replied. "The Queen Charlotte Islands were heavily forested, until they were systematically exploited, with steep cliffs plunging down to the sea."

"The white government didn't really want us competing with

white people even for domestic jobs, Dear. Those jobs were needed for the lower white classes immigrating to Canada."

"So much for the lie of Assimilation," Paul commented.

"We didn't fit in with our families when we returned to the reservation, either. Many of our parents turned to alcohol when their children were taken for the schools and their protests were ignored. The Residential School Clergy had indoctrinated us to be ashamed of our parents and our culture. The repression of sex and the total regimentation in the schools led many to promiscuity and rebellion once students were free. To cope with the extremely negative self-concept the clergy left us with many turned to alcohol and even whatever drugs were available at the time to lessen the pain."

"It must have been impossible to achieve a state of what you psychologists call "positive identity achievement, Rachel," Paul remarked.

"We didn't know who we were," Gran confirmed. "Even when we tried to be white and went to cities for employment, rampant discrimination and racism from the whites severely limited access to jobs and places to live. Young women like me became prey for deviants in the back streets of Vancouver. Young men like my brothers became seriously demoralized as they were rebuffed from jobs and ridiculed as lazy Indians. They became prey for the alcohol and drug sellers in the slums to ease their pain."

"The worst thing of all was that when many of the students from the schools eventually had their own children they had been taught no parenting skills. We often raised our children using the controlling, shaming, angry, correcting ways that had been used by Residential School staff. No one seemed capable of love anymore, on the reserves or in the cities, just despair and anger."

"So much for the practice of getting up at dawn to pray to Jesus, and repenting all the time for your sins," Nigel commented.

"That's why we have several generations of people on reserves consumed with drugs and alcohol, suicide, violence, anger and despair," Paul said.

"Exactly, Dear. Several generations of most families of Indian people in this country had no choice but to attend Indian Residential schools. They were powerless to stop their own children being taken for the schools even though they knew what would happen when they went there. It was mandated by the white man's law and the Indian Act."

"That's what happened to my father, isn't it, Gran?" Rachel felt her emotions reaching a level of turmoil she had never before experienced.

Gran grimaced. Tears came into her eyes. "I couldn't stop them from taking your father to the school in Alberni, Rachel," Gran admitted. "That's where he learned that alcohol deadens the pain of low self-worth. He admitted to me later that the boy's Dormitory Supervisor sexually assaulted him the first night he spent in the school and continued to assault him for years. I've never been able to forgive myself."

Rachel put my arms around Gran. Her face was white as chalk. Rachel willed herself to stop thinking of her parents horrible deaths in a car accident caused by her father's drinking. She had only been three years old.

The paddlers took refuge in the comfortable visitor's lounge on the bottom floor of the school. It was the only place in the entire institution that comfortable chairs and chesterfields were present.

"This room is for show," Gran said, trying to pull her self back together. "They bring visitors and parents here to make them think the rest of the school is as comfortable as this."

"How could those sisters be so inhuman?" Rachel questioned. Gran just shrugged her shoulders.

"They're not inhuman, Darling," Nigel argued. Rachel stared at him in surprise. "They're just passing on the way they were conditioned and indoctrinated as they became Sisters."

"Remember," he continued. "Many of those sisters and priests who ran the schools were brought up in religious institutions themselves. I know. I spent some time in a monastery, myself, when I considered becoming a priest."

"The Catholic church preaches that all bodily urges and needs must be devalued so that the soul can move closer to God. Remember how priests and nuns are taught to whip themselves and deny their own urges to establish supremacy over their bodies."

"All that shaming and use of humiliation and punishment we witnessed to force obedience to senseless rules, that's what the Catholic church uses on it's own clergy?"

"Of course, Darling. And the rules aren't senseless to them. Those rules about silence when in the dining room, silence when waiting in line, silence when doing chores. That's what the Catholic church preaches, the Vow of Silence so that you can hear the voice of God within. That's what they teach the priests and nuns to this day. Believe me, I know."

"That makes a great deal of sense," Rachel told Nigel.

"But the practices were exactly the same in many of the Anglican, Methodist and Presbyterian Residential Schools, how do you explain that?" Gran queried.

"Exactly," Paul said. "It's like one of my old Sociology professors said. The Catholic churches borrowed the practices of the Buddhist Monasteries that predated Christianity. They emphasized mortification of the body. The Protestant churches when they broke away from Rome borrowed the practices of the Catholic churches. The Protestant churches taught their clergy and their parishioners the same principles, that the more they sacrificed and denied their humanity the closer they would be to God. This indoctrination was passed on to Indian students."

"The toxic shame we all learned in Residential schools was not deliberate?" Gran asked.

"It was a by-product of the assumption of white superiority, religious conditioning and indoctrination," Paul claimed. "Just as the neglect, over-correction, anger and shame the children of our people suffered at the hands of their parents whose upbringing had been in Residental Indian Schools was not deliberate."

Rachel suddenly had a thought that shook her up completely. "You don't suppose there's any sexual abuse going on with these poor kinds in the dormitories here, do you? The dormitories here seem to be under unusual security."

""Molestation and sex abuse didn't always happen in the dormitories, Dear," Gran said ominously.

"What do you mean Gran?" All of a sudden the comfortable parlor we were in started to revolve. The now-familiar weight of what must have been the time-travel forcefield pressed on their chests again. Rachel tried not to fight against the forces, this time. Suddenly she felt herself flung down on another wooden floor.

"Oh, my God," They heard Gran say in horror. All four of the paddlers had been transported to an infirmary somewhere within the Residential School.

"It's like the infirmary at the Alberni Indian Residential School," Gran's voice had a choked sound. "The cots have drapes around them just like they did when I attended that infernal school."

They glanced around. The four cots in the infirmary were totally surrounded by drapes on metal drape holders. Behind one drape a student was crying softly. Paul pulled open one corner of the drape so that they could look inside. A black robed priest was sitting far too close to the tiny, female, Indian student on the cot. She couldn't have been more than eight years old. The weight of his body was pressing against the student.

"If only I had a camera," Nigel muttured.

"Now, Suzette, don't be such a crybaby," the priest ordered in a soft voice. Keep that up and I'll go comfort Rita on the other cot. She's not a crybaby like you. Rachel noticed one of the priest's hands restraining the girl from getting up off the cot. She gasped in horror as she saw that his other hand was under the child's underwear stroking her private parts.

"Don't cry, I just want to make you forget your pain, that's all," the priest said in a soft voice. His breath was reeking with wine. Paul went for the priest. He tried to shove him and push him off the child but the priest didn't seem to feel anything. Suzette's crying got more pronounced.

"There's nothing we can do, Rachel," Paul said. He held her close as she shook with fury.

"Oh, very well, then," the priest got up from the cot. "You're such a crybaby, Suzette. I'll come back when you're older," he assured her. The child sobbed openly as the priest disappeared into the other student's draped space.

Some kind of forcefield mercifully took the paddlers away from the scene to the parlor downstairs before they could see what the drunken priest did to the other student. They were helpless to do anything.

"That's how one of the teachers got his way with me," Gran said in disgust.

"I tried to hide in the bathtub in my dormitory when I was sick. I filled it full of coats at night and hid in there, any time I got ill, after my first experience in the infirmary."

"You were abused in the infirmary of your school, Gran?" Rachel said in horror.

"At first, Rachel it was only touching in private areas. But when I got older the same teacher finally got his way with me, many times. He was a trusted member of the school staff. No one believed me when I complained. I was strapped severely for lying."

"That's horrible, Gran."

"No more than what is reported to have happened in the Girl's Dormitory of the Alberni school, years later, Rachel, when your mother attended it."

"What happened there, Gran? Rachel cringed as she thought of her own mother. She had been a tiny, little woman."

"Students have confessed, Rachel, that it was easy to bribe the male Dormitory Supervisor. If you gave him a bottle of whisky he would unlock the girl's dormitory door. The girl's Dormitory Supervisor, slept very soundly. Once she started snoring, whoever had bribed the male supervisor could enter the girl's room and terrorize or socialize with whoever they wanted. Complaints were always ignored.'

"That's the school where Arthur Plint, the Dormitory Super-

visor was sentenced to eleven years for repeatedly sexually assault-
ing over sixteen, male students, aged six to thirteen, from 1948 to
1968 wasn't it Martha?" Paul asked.

"That's right, Paul. My son wasn't alive when he finally went
to trial but I'm sure he would have been one of those testifying to
what Plint did to him."

"The sentencing judge called Plint a "sexual terrorist," and the
Residential School System, "a training ground for Pedophilia, didn't
he?" Paul asked.

"You have a good memory, Dear," Gran said.

Suddenly the room started to revolve furiously. The paddlers
lost consciousness quickly as their lungs felt like they were being
savagely pressed seized in some kind of vice.

When Rachel regained consciousness she found herself in a
tent lying on an air mattress next to Gran.

"We must be back in Victoria," she surmised as the dawn broke
through the darkness and she could hear the sound of Paul Archer's
voice summoning paddlers to the food tent for breakfast.

"Nate?" she asked Gran.

"He's still missing, Dear," Gran said sympathetically. Rachel's
stomach and heart filled with pain and nausea. She realised she
had no way to escape the mind-altering experiences that were happening to her.

"We have to get up and continue with the canoe journey, Gran."

"That's right, Rachel. We need to record the history."

"This gathering of the canoes in Bella Bella, is important, isn't
it, Gran," Rachel asked. She could feel the belief system she had
formulated through her university training cracking further.

"This journey is a way to convince opponents of the Land
Claims that the great majority of Natives in this Province agree on
what they want, Dear."

Rachel nodded. She noted that Gran had an odd expression
on her face. Rachel realised that their experiences in the Residential school had brought back no end of pain for her grandmother.

"I suspect that Raven has more to teach both of us, Rachel."

CHAPTER 7

Interference

Rachel shivered in the food tent as she and Gran sat down beside Paul Archer and Nigel Kent near the back. The weather remained as dry and sunny as Rachel had ever seen it in July but her body felt cold and without warmth. She felt demoralized. She was experiencing the shattering of her belief systems. The complete condemnation of everything Native that they had witnessed in the residential Indian school was causing Rachel to question all the assumptions she possessed.

"I always knew there was some racism operating in white culture against us," she mused. "I've experienced some of it myself. But I never realised it was that bad in Residential schools. No wonder Natives across this country complain about Institutional Racism.

"And it's not something you can blame on long ago," she mused. "Residential schools were in existence in this province as late as the nineteen eighties."

Rachel felt sick. "I thought everything was better now," Rachel mused. "That the governments and the professionals were taking care of everything. That the answer to every problem was more education. How naive of me."

Paul and Nigel were looking very serious as they sat chatting at the back of the food tent. Nigel gave Martha and Rachel a big wave and motioned for them to join himself and Paul.

"At least we all came back this time, Gran."

Gran nodded. Rachel's depressed mood continued. She was

even beginning to doubt the relevance of her own university contributions.

"Take my Doctoral thesis," Rachel acknowledged. "It's a statistical analysis of the efficacy of Crisis Centres for those contemplating suicide. And there's no aboriginal people among the case studies. How could I think I could generalize it's findings to First Nations populations?"

"I'm going to need professional counselling myself if this keeps up. I was so brainwashed by those Psychology professors. Even Paul is laughing at me." Rachel realised she was in the middle of a huge growth period. A shiver went through her body. She felt like an ice crystal.

"You would think I would be used to being alone," she mused. "After all, I haven't dated anyone since Nate left. I've just concentrated on my studies."

"Better put on one of your wool sweaters, Dear," Gran commented noticing her shivers.

"I can't imagine why I'm freezing all the time," Rachel complained. Paul quickly took off his jacket and placed it on her shoulders, giving her a hug. "Thanks, Paul," Rachel sat down beside him.

"God, I'm losing it, now, myself," she acknowledged as emotions kept whirling in her head. "And I prided myself on being psychologically stable."

"Magnificent dancing in the Songhees' longhouse last night, Martha?"

Rachel was glad Nigel was taking over the conversation. She felt her head reeling again as she tried to make sense of all that had happened.

"Indeed, Nigel," Gran replied. "The resurgence of Native culture in British Columbia is one of the most promising things to happen to our people in the last one hundred years. I can feel the ancestors watching with approval."

"And to think that I got that whole ceremonial on video. How fortunate. By the way, my dear, do you suppose you might tell me some of the meaning behind those chants? I'm afraid I was completely carried away by the visual splendour of the whole thing, and missed any of the English explanations that were given."

"I'd be glad to Nigel," Gran replied. "Have you finished your breakfast? Let's go down to the canoes. I'll explain while we wait for the others."

Nigel and Gran went out of the tent.

"Rachel?" She leaned close to catch Paul Archer's whispered words. He had a very serious look on his face.

"Nigel warned me not to speak about what happened to us, when the others are around. I agree."

"Of course, Paul." Rachel lowered her voice to a whisper.

"Do you still think that Martha's explanation of what's going on is balony?"

"No," Rachel found herself admitting ruefully. "Gran says that it's partly because I need to understand the history if I'm going to do drug and alcohol counselling in the coastal villages. After our tour of that Residential School I can see why."

"That's some education you're getting, Rachel, if yesterday was anything like the other time you were back in the past."

"That's what Gran says, Paul? But I wish these crazy happenings would stop. They're making me feel really ashamed of the small amount of European blood in my veins from my great-grandfather. And I feel so helpless when I see the treatment of our people. I seem to be having an enormous growth period. Aren't you feeling the same thing."

Paul smiled. "Oh, as I told you, Rachel, I'm an activist from way back. But I can see now why our people on Kuper Island are so angry at their Residential School. I was there not too long ago when they threw all that remains from the Kuper Island Residential School, the memorial stone, into the sea. Accompanied by drumming, chanting and the cheers of half the population of the Island. That school must have been a lot like the one we viewed."

"Why did you become an activist, Paul?"

"That's how I got over my anger at the racism that occurred to me and the people around me when I was growing up."

"Must one become an activist, Paul? To cope with the history? I don't believe in violence." Paul laughed.

"Being an activist helps coping with the history, Rachel. At least you feel you're doing something to change the way future generations of First Nations' children are treated. But activism doesn't always involve using violence, you know."

"It doesn't?"

"No, the activist techniques I've been taught involve using non-violent passive resistance. Like blocking logging and resource development on lands in the claims areas. And taking advantage of litigation. What we saw yesterday does validate my own conclusions about what happened to our people, though."

"What do you mean, Paul?"

"We lived in poverty in Masset, Rachel, "Paul recounted. "In a house fourteen feet by twenty, without running water. The house had seventeen people in it. My father attended residential school and he was not able to emotionally express himself very well. He became a workaholic rather than an alcoholic but he was financially ruined like so many of the Masset people when the systematic logging of the Queen Charlotte forests wiped out the salmon spawning grounds north of Graham Island that he and so many others fished. They didn't have the big bucks necessary to purchase the large boats they use in the open ocean."

"You became an activist, then, Paul?"

"Later, Rachel. It was when I was feeling really down. When they integrated the schools in Masset and we attended white schools the putdowns all of us experienced made me feel really depressed. The material depravity we lived with became only too apparent when we compared our homes with the white homes that had been built for the white people who came to extract our resources. When two of my sisters were lured into alcohol addiction, by sailors on the Naval Base near Masset, it destroyed my mother. They say she died of Diabetes but I think it was a broken heart."

"That's awful, Paul."

"When I joined the logging blockage on Deer Island, Rachel,

one of the activists finally explained what was happening to our people to me using new words, and finally it made sense to me."

"New words, Paul?"

"Right. Like institutional racism by a dominant culture. Marginalization of the people of the devalued culture. Systematic exploitation of resources. Words like elitism, paternalism, conflicting world views, capitalism without responsibility. Fortunately the guy that taught me those words also convinced me that the only way out of the morass was to get educated. Become a lawyer or something that would help our people. I got so angry I did better in school."

"You managed to get high enough marks to get admitted to university?"

"Right, and when I was admitted to university down here I devoured every history book I could get my hands on. You can't read our history and not come to the conclusion that the English colonizers took our land and all our resources and systematically oppressed and marginalized our people, Rachel. Right up to to-day."

Rachel felt her mind reeling even more. Paul's words rang true after what she had seen.

"I studied the wrong thing, Paul," she blurted. "All those years. I should have studied Political Science instead of Psychology."

"Don't worry about that, Rachel," Paul told her. "Our people are going to need informed professionals from amongst us. When the land claims are settled in this province. Your degrees will give you an in, believe me. And think of how happy some little, native kid is going to be when he looks into the eyes of one of his own people in one of our clinics instead of some disapproving member of a professional elite of a different race."

"That's why these flashbacks are happening to me, Paul? Be-cause I'm going to be a psychologist? But why did something hap-pen to Nate?"

"Whatever happened to Nate may not be connected to the flashbacks, Rachel," Paul warned. "It may be more connected to the death threats Clarissa received at the start of the voyage."

"I don't want to think about that Paul," Rachel moved the conversation elsewhere.

"I wish I knew more about the land claims," she changed the conversation. "I know there's progress with them but I haven't paid much attention to it. I've been too busy working on my Doctorate."

"We'd better get a move on, Rachel," Paul suddenly noticed that the food tent was empty. By the time they got to the beach most of the paddlers were already chanting in the cleansing circle with Martha McBay.

After the ceremonies were over Paul and Rachel jumped into the second seat behind Gran and the five canoes moved off in unison.

Rachel felt her spirits pick up slightly as she and the other paddlers moved the canoes out of the bay and towards Chemainus, their destination for the day. The sun was hot and Rachel soon removed her sweater.

"Surely we'll be all right now," she thought. "With five canoes we can always pick up everyone if one of the canoes capsizes. Nate will make it back if he can, I know. And Paul Archer is one of the most knowledgeable men I have ever met."

Rachel glanced over at Paul's left hand. No wedding band was on his ring finger.

"I wonder if he has a significant other?" Rachel found herself thinking.

The day passed quickly with Gran and Ernie Alfred putting on a show of drumming and chanting all the way. By the time the canoes made it to Chemainus, the sun was about to disappear into the sea. Paul spotted the signal fire for the reserve they were scheduled to stay on for the night.

The paddlers steered the canoes in the direction of the fire. Then suddenly Rachel spotted something that made shivers go up her spine. A fishing boat from near the shore was coming towards the canoes at full speed. There was something about the boat that looked familiar.

"Paul, that fishboat!" she shouted, as cold fear shot through her body. "That's the same one that was moving towards Nate in Neah Bay."

The paddlers stared at the boat rapidly approaching to the right of the canoes. It was an old fishing boat with a two-tone white and grey paint job. A red stripe around the mid-ships separated the two colours from each other.

"Jesus, that guy doesn't seem to see us," Ernie shouted. Paul reached for a large battery-powered light on the floor of the canoe and flashed it rapidly several times at the boat. The boat made no move to divert. It's owner seemed to be aiming right at the lead canoe.

"It's the same poles, Paul," Rachel shouted. She stared at the trawler's long poles behind the wheelhouse. The setting sun was reflecting off of them. "Something on the poles is florescent, just like the poles on the boat that headed for Nate. I remember the sun flashing off them in Neah Bay."

"Mother Jesus," shouted Nigel. "Get out of that front seat, Martha," he ordered. "That boat is headed right for us at top speed." Gran scrambled backwards into Rachel and Paul's seat, then crawled over them as Nigel grabbed her and pulled her back with him.

"Let's get out of here," Ernie yelled.

"There's no time," Paul answered. The fishboat was advancing rapidly towards them. It's old motor sounded like it was going to fly to bits at any moment.

Paul waved to the other four canoes to disburse. They all moved off in different directions. The fishboat kept coming towards Paul's canoe.

"When I yell, paddle to starboard," Paul shouted, pointing to all the paddlers on the starboard side.

Rachel realised he was going to try and dodge the fish boat at the last moment. Intense fear shot through her heart at the desperateness of their situation.

The paddlers in the canoe had no choice but to stare at the advancing boat with increasing horror. A large figure in the wheelhouse could be seen as the boat closed in on their canoe. Yellow raingear masked any recognizable features. Rachel realised that the fishboat's name and serial numbers were blocked off.

"Now," Paul yelled as the boat bore down on them. Rachel threw her paddle into the sea on the starboard side joining the others in frantically pulling through the water. She was leaning forward and to the right. Rachel felt the canoe swerve just as the fishboat struck it.

There was a sickening crunch and the sound of wood splitting. Rachel screamed as a blast of pain shot through her right side. The canoe had been dealt a glancing blow by the fishboat. Part of the front had broken off and struck Rachel.

The roar of the fishboat's motor deafened Rachel's ears.

The force of the impact sent some paddlers flying into the water. The canoe itself flipped over spewing out the paddlers still able to clutch on. The cold of the water made Rachel gasp. Rachel heard the roar of the fishboat's motor lessen.

"Thank God it's not coming back for another charge," she thought.

"Mother Jesus," she heard Nigel shout. "There's something wrong with Rachel!"

Rachel realised her right arm and leg were not working properly. She was face down in the water and having difficulty holding her head up. Somehow she rolled onto her back and frantically paddled with her one functioning arm trying to keep afloat. Excruciating pain was shooting through her right arm and side.

"My God, I'm going to die," she thought. She could feel herself tiring rapidly and starting to sink down in the water. She tried desperately to hold her breath as her head sunk below the surface. Rachel went into a full-blown panic.

"This is it," her mind registered. Rachel couldn't breathe or speak. She gagged and choked as she finally opened her mouth gasping for air. Water flooded in. She swallowed in desperation. Water made its way into her lungs.

Suddenly strong arms grabbed her from below and forced her up out of the water. Rachel gasped and choked as she tried to bring up the water trapped in her lungs and nose.

"Don't worry, Rachel, I've got you," Paul Archer shouted breathlessly as Rachel went into convulsions. She looked up as air finally managed to reach her lungs. The last thing she remembered was the sight of the old fishboat that had rammed them moving eerily in the distance out towards open sea like some white and grey ghost ship.

Paul Archer managed to keep Rachel's head above the water long enough for one of the other canoes to reach them.

"Be careful," he warned as he passed Rachel's limp body to others in the canoe. "She's been injured on the right side."

"What's that?" One of the paddlers pointed to an object floating in the water.

"Oh, God!" Paul Archer gasped. "Someone's been killed." The light was dimming but Paul realised with horror that he was viewing a body floating face down on top of the water.

"Gran!" Rachel woke up screaming in her hospital bed. "Gran!" sheer terror was evident in the young woman's voice.

"It's OK Rachel," Martha McBay rushed to Rachel's side from the chair she had been sitting in. "You're all right now, It's OK, Darling." Rachel stared as Gran put her arms around her left arm and body and hugged her as best she could.

"Gran, the canoe?" Rachel gasped.

"It's gone to the bottom of the sea, Rachel, but don't worry, you're not seriously hurt." Nigel Kent was standing behind Gran.

Rachel stared at the bandages on her right arm and side. She moved her arm. It obeyed her command but only at the price of excruciating pain.

"Don't worry, Darling," Nigel assured her. "Nothing's broken. You've got a bad sprain and several broken ribs. Plus miscellaneous scrapes and bruises but nothing life-threatening. They say it must have been the paddling you've done that saved you. The muscle mass on your upper arms, shoulders and back prevented serious injury."

"Paul saved us," Rachel said. "All of us in the canoe."

"Indeed he did, Darling. Brilliant reacting on his part, if you ask me. The dugout glanced off the fishboat when the canoe swerved. That bastard running that boat was only able to smash a piece of the front off the canoe not plough right over us like he wanted to. Unfortunately the piece that broke off seems to have hit you."

Rachel stared at her grandmother. She was pale as a ghost and her hands were shaking.

"What's wrong, Gran?" Rachel demanded.

Gran took Rachel's left hand firmly in her own.

"Brace yourself, Dear," Gran's voice shook with pain.

"Nate Archer is dead, Rachel," Nigel told her as Gran's voice faltered.

"No," Rachel cried out. Gran held her as well as she could with the injuries.

"His body was thrown from that fishboat, Rachel as it moved away from us," Nigel continued. "Nate must have been held captive on it all this time. A single shot had been fired into his head and there were bruises on his body from a struggle. The police say it must have happened just before the boat made it's attack on us."

"Nigel, call the nurse," Gran ordered.

Rachel had gone into fits of crying.

"She needs a sedative," Nigel explained as a white-coated nurse came running into the room.

The nurse nodded and rushed out of the room. Minutes later Rachel felt her intense pain end as she lost consciousness. A needle had been inserted into her veins.

"She'll be out till morning, now," the nurse said sympathetically to Martha McBay.

"There's nothing you can do, tonight, Darling," Nigel put his arms around Rachel's grandmother and pulled her towards the door.

"Stay with me, Nigel, will you?" It was all Martha McBay could do to stagger towards the door.

"Of course, Darling." Nigel used his strength to keep Martha on her feet.

"It's going to be all right, Martha," he tried to reassure her as they walked along long corridors out to the lobby. Paul Archer was waiting for them in the lobby.

"I've got a car outside," he said sympathetically, noting the way Martha McBay was looking.

"Anything new Paul?" Nigel asked.

"The RCMP and Coast Guard are searching for that boat, Nigel. But do you know how many white and grey fishing trawlers there are on this coast. How's Rachel?"

"She's not badly injured, Paul, but she's taking Nate Archer's death hard. The nurse knocked her out with a sedative."

"Drive Martha back to the reserve, Nigel,"

Paul ordered. "I'll stay here until Rachel wakes up." He gave some car keys to Nigel. "It's the blue Blazer out in the emergency parking lot."

CHAPTER 8

The Aftermath

"The poles behind the wheelhouse, they've got something florescent on them," Rachel said as she regained consciousness and recognized Paul Archer staring at her from a chair.

"That was the same fishboat that came in to pick up Nate," Rachel gasped.

"I know, Rachel. The RCMP are searching for it. Just take it easy, all that can be done is being done, believe me," Paul advised.

"Nate's body?" Rachel gasped.

"It's going to be flown back to Bella Bella, Rachel. As soon as the autopsy is finished. Nate's parents are arranging the funeral."

"I have to go up there."

"No, Rachel. You need to heal."

"Oh, God! Paul, this isn't going to stop the voyage, is it? Nate wouldn't want that to happen."

"No, Rachel."

Paul let Rachel cry openly for several minutes. Then, when she had managed some control he filled Rachel in on the latest developments. He told her how Clarissa and the others were more determined than ever now. And that the date for the gathering was being changed as well as the official route of the canoes. For security reasons.

Paul told her that Clarissa was coming down with one of her husband's fishboats to act as an escort vessel for the paddlers. And that Clarissa was towing another dugout canoe she had located from Bella Bella.

"We're all flying up for the funeral," Paul explained. "By the time we're ready to proceed again you'll be physically as good as new, believe me."

"I'll never be quite the same again, Paul," Rachel answered.

"You and Paul were once engaged to be married, Rachel? Had you two got close again? Forgive me if I'm being too forward?"

"Oh, it's all right, Paul. Nate and I broke off years ago. And with Nate, it was mostly physical," Rachel admitted. I don't think we had all that much else in common. Nate wanted to talk. That's the last thing he said to me."

"Rachel, remember we need to talk, he said, just before Gran, Nigel and I were returned to the present. But I think he just wanted to apologise for breaking off our engagement so abruptly." Paul hugged her as she broke into tears again.

"You know, Paul, I think Nate sensed that he wasn't going to live very long. He seemed to be trying to get things taken care of before he died, like any hard feelings from our breakup."

"I've heard of experiences like that, Rachel. If I can be of any help, by the way," he offered. "In any way?"

Rachel managed a wan smile.

"Thanks, Paul," she said.

Rachel spent four days in the hospital and ten days recuperating in Chemainus with Gran.

"You need to stop pacing back and forth like that, Dear," Gran advised after several days. "It's not going to help anyone."

"I know, Gran," Rachel tried to still the depressing and morbid thoughts in her head. "All I can think about is Nate's death. It's so horrible. He must have been trying to stop the attack on the canoes when he was shot."

"You need to get out for a drive, Dear. I'm going to visit an old friend, Lorraine Peters. She's an Elder, on the Cape Mudge reserve. It's a bit of a drive to Campbell River and a ferry ride from there. Why don't you join me?"

"All right, Gran," Rachel agreed. "Anything is better than sitting here, brooding. But I'm not sure I'm going to be good company for you."

"I know how hard it is to get over the death of someone you were close to, Dear, even if it was some years ago." Gran put her arms around her and hugged her close.

"It must have been hard, Gran, when my parents were killed. And when grandfather died not too long after of complications from Diabetes."

"It was, Dear. But something good did turn out of all that tragedy. I finally suffered so much I turned to the healing methods of our people. It was the start of so much learning for me. I joined a women's talking circle in our village and look what that led to."

"I know, Gran. You never stopped after that. You became a living repository for the old culture. Look how much influence you have now."

"It's important to get caught up in something bigger than yourself, Dear. It helps you get out of your own ego, somehow and see the larger picture."

Gran's words kept echoing in Rachel's ears as they travelled over the roads towards the Cape Mudge ferry.

"Gran do they have a women's talking circle on this reserve? I'd like to take part in it if they do."

"I'll ask my friend, Lorraine, Dear, when we get there."

So it happened that Rachel and Gran were invited to the Women's Talking Circle for the Cape Mudge Reserve. It met twice a week and one had already been scheduled for the evening that day.

Rachel wasn't sure what to expect as she, Gran, and Lorraine Peters, walked over to the community hall. She had already received quite a shock in the afternoon. Lorraine, a warm, big-hearted lady who exuded spirituality, like Nigel would say, had taken them to the Cape Mudge Museum shortly after their arrival.

The artifacts looked strangely familiar to Rachel.

"Gran, we've seen these masks before," she commented. Gran stared at the regalia, masks and coppers displayed in a large glass case in the main display section of the museum.

"Indeed we have," Gran gasped.

"Oh, you couldn't have," Lorraine told them. "Unless you've been to our museum before. Those are the regalia, masks and coppers confiscated by Indian Agent William Halliday in 1922 from one of our potlatches on Village Island and sent to a museum in Ottawa. They were not returned to us until 1979, when one of our chiefs made some inquiries in high places. We built this museum to celebrate the return of the artifacts."

"Some masks and regalia are missing," Rachel stated, describing some of the masks she had seen at the 1921 Potlatch.

"How did you know that?" Lorraine demanded. Our Indian Agent, William Halliday sold some of the collection to an American museum. Those artifacts were never recovered."

Gran just winked at Lorraine. "Some things are best left unsaid, Dear."

Rachel wasn't sure just what would happen at the woman's talking circle. Gran had told her some of the protocol after dinner.

"It's not like one of your group therapy sessions, Dear," Gran had warned. "A talking circle is totally supportive and confrontation is not allowed. Everyone will be asked to participate as the 'Talking Stick' is passed around but they may pass if they wish. Only the person holding the 'Talking Stick' is allowed to speak. The others must listen."

"Is advice given, Gran?"

"Sometimes if requested, Dear. And it's often the Elder that gives it. But when a question is raised, the members of the circle usually talk of similar problems that happened to them, without specifics of course, and how the problems were solved."

The Cape Mudge Women's Talking Circle was held in a comfortable area of the community hall. Rachel sat down in one of the stuffed armchairs that had been arranged in a circle and tired to calm her raging thoughts. Sorrow at Nate's death, horror at it and the attack on the canoes, anger at whoever had committed the murder, and self-blame surged through her mind.

"We never did get to have that talk Nate wanted," Rachel

sobbed to herself. "He never did get to clear up whatever it was he wanted to say to me."

Rachel tried to stop her thoughts as Lorraine Peters started the circle. Gran's old friend lit a smudge in an ashtray and moved it through the four corners of the room. One of the ladies from the reserve chanted some ancient chant. Another drummed in rhythm to the chanting.

"That's to get rid of any negativity that might be present," Gran whispered. Rachel felt the pain around her heart lighten up somewhat.

She glanced around at the others in the room. They seemed a warm, friendly, lot. Fifteen women, aged from around her age all the way to Gran's gave them welcoming smiles.

"Don't tell them what I'm becoming in university, Gran, Rachel had warned. "I don't want them thinking I'm an expert or something."

"Just tell them you're a student, Dear. You don't have to elaborate."

Rachel watched and listened closely as Lorraine gave a talk to start the session off.

"For those of you who are new to the Talking Circle this is our 'Talking Stick,' she explained. Lorraine held up a beautiful piece of Kwakiutl art.

"This Talking Stick is made out of cedar. Cedar is for cleansing," Lorraine continued. "I have others made out of other woods for different purposes. Only the person holding the Talking Stick is allowed to speak," she warned. "Others must listen carefully. This is the 'Answer Feather.' Only the person holding the 'Answer Feather' is allowed to respond.

Lorraine held onto the 'Talking Stick' as she gave an opening prayer. Rachel was surprised to hear her ask for the ladies to pray for the benefit of all the earth's creatures not just themselves, including the 'four leggeds,' the 'plant people' and the 'stone people.' After the prayer Lorraine gave a brief teaching about 'Great Mystery,' who she called the 'Original Source of Creation,' and who contains 'All That Is.' Lorraine explained how many people commonly confused 'Great Mystery' with the 'Great Spirit'. She told the members of the circle that 'Great Spirit' was created by 'Great Mystery,' to oversee the direction of the universes for 'Great Mystery.'

"The mistake that many make," Lorraine continued. "is to think that they have to solve the nature of 'Great Mystery.' That is beyond our comprehension as 'Great Mystery' contains ourselves as well," she warned. "As a 'two-legged', one must try and understand only what are your unique talents, and choose a path in life so that you can do the best that you are capable of and along with the help of the 'Great Spirit,' contribute to the benefit of all the clans and all the creatures on your 'Earth Walk.'

Rachel was stunned. She had never allowed Gran to speak to her about much of the old ways.

"I never thought that Native spirituality was so profound," she mused.

Lorraine ended her teaching and announced that it was time to pass around the 'Talking Stick' to those of the circle who wanted to bring up a matter of importance to them or to share some experience for the benefit of all. Rachel went into shock as Lorraine handed her the 'Talking Stick.'

"Hello, I'm Rachel McBay from Bella Bella," she managed. "I feel quite honoured to be with you here tonight." Suddenly Rachel's voice faltered as she felt quite overcome by sorrow. "Perhaps some of you can help me," she gasped. "Someone to whom I was once very close passed away lately." Tears came to Rachel's eyes. "Quite unexpectedly," she added. "At quite a young age."

Lorraine Peters nodded. She handed the 'Answer Feather' to one of the ladies who raised her hand.

"I'm Phyllis Mackie, and I understand what you are going through Rachel," a lady who looked like she was in her forties, spoke. "I lost my sixteen year old son only two years ago. He laid his physical body down on the Malahat Highway one, wet night and waited there until a trailer tractor ran over him in the darkness. I blamed myself for his death."

"Would you like to tell us exactly what had led to his suicide," asked Lorraine who still held the 'Talking Stick.'

"I didn't realise he believed all the negative things that people that were telling him. Like that he was a loser, had no hope of making it in school, and that he'd always be a lazy Indian. And I didn't believe him when he told me he was being sexually assaulted by his uncle."

Rachel felt an enormous grief emanating from the lady with the 'Answer Feather.' It matched her own.

"I suffered so much from self-guilt that I finally went to the women's talking circle' in the village I lived in before I came to Cape Mudge," Phyllis continued. "It took me awhile but I finally came to realise that my son really didn't end completely. That he just changed worlds. That his 'Earthwalk' was over this time but that there would likely be others."

"Some good came from the death, Phyllis?" Lorraine prompted.

"Yes, my family took advantage of the First Nations trained sex abuse workers available on our reserve and explored the patterns of sexual abuse that had been amongst us ever since so many of us attended the Alberni Indian Residential School. Even my son's uncle who had assaulted him came forward, admitted his crime, showed remorse and tried to make amends."

Rachel felt her head spinning from Phylis's words.

"Some good is coming out of Nate's death, too," she realised. "His death had made everyone connected to the canoe journey more determined than ever to carry on. It had the opposite affect than whoever is carrying out these ghastly attacks hoped for. Who knows, maybe that's all that can be expected from some lives, that others benefit somehow from what happened with yours."

A few of the other ladies told their stories of how they had coped with death in their families. They all emphasized that with time the pain of the survivors lessened. Surprisingly, some good seemed to have come from all the deaths.

"Remember, it's important to have compassion," Lorraine Peters closed the session. She ended the session with a prayer for the benefit of all creatures and people on the planet.

"I hope that was some help, Dear," Gran questioned Rachel as they took the ferry back from Quadra Island.

"I feel a little more at peace, now, Gran," Rachel sighed. "If only whoever killed Nate is found. I know I should pray even for the murderer, too, like Lorraine says, but that's going to take more time, I think."

By the time the paddlers returned from the funeral in Bella Bella and were ready to continue their journey the only visible evidence of Rachel's injuries was the black and yellow bruising on her right arm and side. All the paddlers were given the choice of continuing on the journey or accepting replacement by other volunteers from their nations. Not one of the paddlers chose to give up.

Paul Archer drew Rachel off by herself as she and Gran turned up on the beach at Chemainus for the continuation of the Voyage of Solidarity.

"Rachel, good to see you," he said warmly as he gave her a long hug.

"I want to thank you, Paul," Rachel hugged him back. "You saved me from drowning. If you hadn't reached me when you did I would have been a goner for sure."

"Someone else would have reached you, Rachel. Sure you want to go on with this, by the way?" he asked.

"You couldn't pay me enough to quit now. Imagine some crazy person willing to commit murder to stop us from demonstrating solidarity for the land claims negotiations."

"Don't be so sure it's a lunatic we're dealing with, Rachel. "There's lots of people who have a vested interest in derailing these negotiations."

"No luck in finding the fishboat?"

"The RCMP are working on it but they haven't got much to go on. No one's come forward to claim responsibility or make further threats."

"Poor Nate," Rachel choked. "His parents must have been so upset."

People came for all over the province for the funeral, Rachel. Even some of the First Nations Tribal Groups that were completely against the treaty talks are considering taking part, now. And some of my friends in the movement are thinking of going after that murderer themselves. "

There's a special task force on this Paul. They'll get to the bottom of it, I'm sure."

"Perhaps. In the meantime we're going to have Clarissa, herself, escorting us all the way up the coast." Paul pointed at a large fishing boat moored out in the harbor.

"Hope that bastard comes for us again," he said. "Clarissa's got a high-powered gun used to finish elephants off. She'll blow him out of the water if he even gets into the range of that gun."

Rachel nodded. She and Paul sat down on a log. The others were loading gear into the canoes. Rachel managed a weak smile as she saw Nigel Kent load what looked like a large, underwater video camera capable of floating into their dugout. He and Gran were carrying on an animated conversation.

"Tell me some of the history of the Land Claims, Paul," Rachel requested as it looked like it was going to be a little while before everything was ready for departure.

"Oh, no," Rachel suddenly called out as the part of the beach they were sitting on started to revolve.

"Not so soon," she begged. Rachel felt herself losing consciousness as the spinning seemed to cause excruciating pain in her right arm and side.

"It's like something was listening to our conversation," she managed as a weight on her lungs forced all the oxygen out of them. She gasped as her sight dimmed.

CHAPTER 9

Metlatakla

"Paul, are you all right?" I shook my head as I could hear Rachel McBay calling me from far away. I tried to focus but my eyes were not obeying my commands.

"Pull yourself into a sitting position, Paul," she commanded. I managed to pull myself up with her help.

"Where are we, this time Rachel?" I asked as I felt cold and wetness seeping through my clothes.

I felt around me and realised that I was lying on the dock of a huge shed. I realised from the way Rachel was dressed that we were back in the past again. She was wearing a long, deep red, velvet dress appropriate for the Victorian era. I couldn't help but notice that she looked quite lovely in it.

I glanced at my clothes. They looked like they came from the late 1800's.

"We're in Metlatakla, Dear," Martha McBay's voice informed me. I glanced past Rachel and realised both Nigel Kent and Rachel's grandmother were behind us on a dock.

"What an education!" I thought. "To personally experience the happenings of the past. My heart pounded. My mind gave up thinking about Nate Archer's death.

"These flashbacks are validating my choice to become an activist." I thought, "something I'm not always sure of even though I always put on a strong front to others. And Rachel's here, too. Quite a lady, even if she's not into activism. Going on with the canoe journey after all she went through. What courage."

"Metlatakla, Darling?" Nigel inquired.

"The settlement that Mr. William Duncan created, Nigel. In the 1860's near Fort Simpson," Martha commented.

I recalled what I had read about the history of Metlatakla. Metlatakla was an all out attempt by the Tsimshian people to assimilate in the 1860's with the people that had invaded their lands.

I glanced around the huge storage shed we were in front of. Something seemed odd. There were several more large wooden sheds in view as well as a dry dock for boat repair. I could see a sawmill, and some kind of industrial building but they appeared to be completely abandoned. The doors and windows were missing from the storage shed and the contents had been removed.

"This must be after the exodus," I reasoned, remembering the history again. We must have arrived here just after the seven hundred Tsimshian followers of William Duncan went with him to Alaska. From the looks of the subdivision up the hill. All the doors and windows have been removed. Even from the church.

I couldn't believe what I was witnessing. An entire village, looking for all life that it had been transported from Victorian England, stood on the hill above the dry dock and storage sheds. A huge, frame church, loomed over the scenery. On each side of the church, large, European designed, two-storied frame houses, complete with white picket fences, stood linked together by wooden walkways.

I gasped. Even lamp posts stood at measured distances along the streets. What looked like a school and a store were visible from the dock we stood on. But only a few people were visible in the entire village. They were walking around staring at the missing doors and windows.

Martha McBay led the way up to the centre of the complex. It was eery. No one could see us or hear us. I felt like I was in the middle of a newly-created ghost town.

"Where are all the community longhouses?" Rachel asked. "And the totems, like we saw at Alert Bay and Village Island."

"William Duncan had any community houses here taken down, Rachel and the totems destroyed." I volunteered. "He was determined like the other Anglican and Methodist missionaries from England to turn our people into imitation, Victorian, English working class people."

Pictures of the Metlataklan women, dressed in Victorian English dresses down to their ankles, with their hair parted in the middle and tied back in buns came into my mind. The ladies were crouched over looms, weaving wool in one of the pictures of the history books I had read. And their sons were dressed in English military uniforms playing hymns on the trumpets, french horns and drums of William Duncan's brass band.

"What a dark day in our history," I thought. All those totems and art objects destroyed. For all the good it did the Metlataklans."

"How did the Tsimsian people wind up here?" Rachel questioned. "I thought they were located closer to Fort Simpson."

"Mr. Duncan moved some of the Tsimshian here from Fort Simpson when they turned to him during one of the small pox epidemics that was wiping out one/third of the natives in British Columbia, Rachel," I told her. "William Duncan would only vaccinate those Tsimshian that agreed to abandon their old ways and settle with him here in Metlatakla. He was determined to isolate them. Make them give up their spirituality and culture, and turn them into carbon copies of English, Victorian. working class people."

I recalled that by 1886, when the Metlataklans went to Alaska, many of the Tsimsian people living in Metlatakla spoke English and all worked in the salmon cannery, sawmill and cottage industries that William Duncan had set up. Their children attended his school, already learning English and losing their language. Duncan even had one of the first Indian girl's homes going, complete with severe physical punishment for disobedience."

"What's happened here Darling?" Nigel demanded.

"These people moved to Alaska, Nigel," Martha told him. "In the late 1880's, the white Federal and Provincial governments wouldn't even guarantee that the land the houses stood on at Metlatakla would be put into a reserve for the people. And the elected village council, which governed the community, felt threatened when it was going to be placed under the direction of an Indian Agent."

"Native people's homes were on the very land that the white settlers, land speculators, government officials, and railroad people wanted for themselves, the sites of the future cities of the Province," I added.

"Exactly, Paul," Martha McBay agreed.

"So no matter how well the First Nations people's brass bands played the Christian hymns, or how similar the First Nation's people dressed, lived, talked and worked like their Victorian white, working class, counterparts, they would never be accepted as equals into the white world. They could not even get title to their own land or control of their own resources."

I recalled that once the Metlataklans realised that they would never be accepted as equals in the white world of British Columbia they negotiated the American offer of squatters rights on Annette Island in Alaska and resettled there with William Duncan.

"So much for the lie of Assimilation that propelled the Residential School System," Rachel gasped.

Suddenly the boardwalk that we all were standing on started to revolve suddenly. I threw myself down trying not to fight the force-field that was enveloping us. When the spinning stopped I found myself lying on my back on a beach somewhere. Wetness was seeping though my pantlegs. I glanced at my clothes. I was still wearing the clothes from Metlatakla. I carefully moved my hands and legs to see if I could get back some feeling in my limbs.

The sound of raucous sea gulls crying pulled me away from my thoughts. Then I heard the sound of paddles being pulled rhythmically through water.

"Get up, Paul. You've got to move," Rachel ordered. "Some dugout canoes are moving right towards us. I don't imagine the men in them can see you lying here."

I turned at Rachel's words. My eyes cleared as I focused on the water. Rachel was right. Three large dugout canoes were heading right for where I was lying. I looked back at Rachel and realised that Martha McBay and Nigel Kent were behind her.

Nigel gave me a hand and with his help I managed to pull myself up onto my feet.

"Go over there," Martha McBay directed. "Beside that other man waiting on the beach."

Nigel helped me stagger over to a log on the shoreline. I sat down beside someone dressed in formal dress. He didn't seem to see us or hear us. The fellow on the log, Nigel and I were in three piece suits but the way they were cut was very different from twentieth century suits. Rachel and Martha were in dresses down to their ankles and if I was not mistaken wearing tight-fitting corsets that made their waists look tiny.

"We're still in the late 1800's, I think," I remarked to Martha McBay.

"I hope we won't be here long, Dear," Martha McBay commented. "Corsets like these haven't been worn for over one hundred years, thank God. I can hardly breathe."

"Welcome gentleman," our well-dressed man shouted out to the people in the dugouts who were exiting the canoes. "Premier Smithe is waiting for you in his parlor. Allow me to direct you to his house."

"Thank you Dr. Powell," one of the native fellows in the canoe answered.

I remembered a Dr. Israel Wood Powell from my studies. He was the first Indian Commissioner in British Columbia under the Federal Indian Act.

"Raven must be showing us what happened to the other Tsimshian, the ones that didn't go to New Metlatakla in Alaska," Martha McBay commented.

"Oh, good, you're here, Chief Barton, we need a translator," Dr. Powell commented.

"Surely our minister, Reverend Thomas Crosby, can translate. My English is not so good," Chief Barton protested.

"It will have to do, Chief Barton. Reverend Crosby was told not to come to the meeting. The Premier wants to hear from the Chiefs directly without any white interpreter present, particularly if they are a Methodist Minister. Quite frankly, I'm afraid Premier Smithe thinks your Methodist missionaries have put words in your mouths. And he thinks the missionaries are behind the unrest up at Fort Simpson, in the Nishga'a region and here on the South Coast."

Anger filled me at Powell's words. I remembered the history that likely spurred the protest. Despite their small size, reserves in in British Columbia were reduced by Land Commissioner Joseph Trutch in the 1850's following James Douglas' retirement. Trutch had removed many acres of the best reserve land for white pre-emption. White families were allowed to pre-empt one hundred and sixty acres and buy as many more as they could afford. Indians were restricted to ten acres per family despite Federal Government orders to allow them sixty acres.

The presence of white land speculators and government surveyors at Fort Simpson eyeing the waterfront land their houses were on had spooked the Tsimshian. Vancouver Island Indians had been horrified at the selling of one the Songhees' reserves adjacent to Victoria harbor without compensation or consultation with them by Prime Minister John A. MacDonald for $60,000.00 to coal and railroad baron, James Dunsmuir. And that was after assuring a delegation of Tsimshian Chiefs to Ottawa that he would look out for their interests.

Dr. Powell looked uncomfortable as Chief Barton complained about these and other injustices.

Powell tried to make excuses about the governments actions. He told Chief Barton that it was difficult for the white government in Victoria to appreciate how far the Tsimshian people had come in such a short time. Powell said that he knew, because of his frequent trips to Fort Simpson and Metlatakla, a few miles away. That he had seen their new European-design houses in subdivisions in Metlatakla and Fort Simpson. And their outstanding, elected, village-councils in action. He told them that the new church they were building would rival even those that were in Victoria itself, and that their European-style brass bands rivaled even that of the Salvation Army in Victoria.

But Powell asked them to understand.

"Understand what, Dr. Powell?" Chief Barton demanded.

Powell told him that people down here in Victoria were only used to interacting with the rather disorderly crowd of drunken natives that come to trade. He said that none of the traders had advanced anywhere near as far or as quickly as the Tsimshians at Fort Simpson.

"Is that true, Paul?" Rachel asked. I snorted.

"No, Rachel. By 1878 the Anglican Reverend Hall had established a model Anglican village at Alert Bay. And the Roman Catholic, Oblate fathers were making as much so-called progress converting the Vancouver Island tribes and Coast Salish people on the mainland as their counterparts in the north, the Methodists and Anglicans, were in Fort Simpson."

I told Rachel how Roman Catholic churches had been built in First Nations villages and similar tactics as William Duncan's were being used to control the people. For example, in Squirrel Cove, a native bell captain was appointed to spy on his people in the absence of the Priest and report any breaking of the church regulations. Punishments for minor violations of church regulations were severe, such as standing for hours with the arms outstretched for throwing rocks at a statue of Christ, or standing with the hands on the head at the front of the Church for arriving late or wearing perfume.

Chief Barton's voice raised voice brought us back to the beach we were all standing on.

"We are spokesmen for our people, Dr. Powell, not mouthpieces for the missionaries that have come to live amongst us. They came at our invitation."

"I know, Chief Barton. I realise the Tsimshian's determination to take their places in the white man's world. The changes you have made to your way of life are laudible. I assure you. But you must understand. Other Indians of this Province have not thrown off their ways as quickly as the Tsimshian. Those are the Indians that the government and people of Victoria are accustomed to."

"We want what was promised to us, Commissioner Powell. We want to be given the same rights as the white people who have come to our land to claim it as their own. We want our title to our lands and control of our fishing and hunting sites as was promised."

"Yes, of course, Gentleman," Powell looked apologetic. "If only Premier Douglas had not retired. His hopes were that Indians would be able to pre-empt the lands as well as the whites. That would have made you all equal. But the present Premier has different ideas, I'm afraid. And he is waiting. Please follow me."

The four men went up the road with Dr. Powell. Their native paddlers stayed with the canoes.

"We had better follow them," Martha McBay said. "Raven wants us to witness this."

"Witness what, Gran?" Rachel asked.

"These are the Tsimshian and Nishga'a Chiefs who came to Victoria in 1887, Rachel, to protest the theft of their land for pre-emption by white settlers up at Fort Simpson and the Nass river valley."

We trailed along behind the Chiefs and within minutes came to the imposing estates and eloborate, woodframe houses of the early settlers of Victoria.

"Why is the Premier meeting the Chiefs here, rather than in the Government offices?" I asked.

"He likely doesn't want witnesses to this interview," Martha McBay replied. "Or anyone attempting to act on the Chief's behalf. I'm sure Premier Smithe has a hidden agenda, just like white governments always have when they meet with our people."

We followed the Chiefs into a very formal parlor furnished with furniture from the Victorian era. A fire was lit in the large stone fireplace and a man who must have been Premier Smithe was sitting looking displeased in a wine-colored, ornate chair. Two other officials were seated in the room as well.

"Sit down," the Premier ordered. The chiefs obliged.

"Allow me to introduce these gentlemen, Premier Smithe?" Dr. Powell asked.

"If you must but let them realise that my Attorney-General Alex Daie, here, and I are granting these Indians an immense favor by meeting with them at all. Particularly after their treatment of Mr. Peter O'Reilly's party of surveyors several months ago. The third offical in the room stood up."

"I'm Peter O'Reilly," he said curtly.

"Peter O'Reilly is the Land Commissioner who systematically toured the province with the intent of reducing the size of Indian reserves," Martha McBay snarled.

"Gentlemen, Dr. Powell looked discomforted. "Remember, you don't want to risk an Indian war up on the North Coast where these gentlemen come from."

"Yes, yes, do proceed." Premier Smith ordered.

"This is Chief Charles Barton of the Nishga'a people. He is going to act as the English interpretor for the others. Allow me to present Chief Richard Wilson of the Tsimshian people and Chiefs Arthur Gurney and John Wesley of the Nishga'a."

"Premier Smithe nodded curtly to Chief Barton."

"Now, Dr. Powell, we'll see what these Indians have to say without their mentors, those infernal Methodist missionaries, doing the talking for them. I trust they are here to apologise for their threats of violence and reprisal that we've been hearing of lately in Victoria. Perhaps we can set these Indians straight about what limited rights they actually have."

"I assure you that that missionary fellow, Thomas Crosby, and that other one, William Duncan, have been filling your heads with delusions."

"You have heard the latest about Mr. Duncan and our brothers at Metlatakla, have you not?" Chief Barton interrupted.

"Yes of course," Smithe answered. He recounted in an angry

voice the exodus of Duncan, the Tsimshian and their sawmill and cannery to Alaska.

"Such impertinence," Smithe commented. "As if the government of the United States treats Indians any better than we do."

"That is one of the reasons we are here, Premier Smithe. We wished your government to escape further shame amongst the world governments similar to what the Metlataklans have caused for you. Many of our Tsimshian brothers at Fort Simpson are thinking of leaving British Columbia and joining the Metlataklans. Unless you assure us that we will be granted title to the land on which we have sacrificed much to build our houses, school and church."

Premier Smithe avoided the question of land title. "The Alaskan Government did offer the Tsimshian at Metlatakla squatting rights on Anette Island, Premier Smithe," Dr. Powell confronted him. "Can't we do something like that for these gentlemen?"

"How can these backward people demand rights of any kind?" Premier Smithe blustered. "And threaten violence and reprisals if they don't get them."

"Those threats of violence and reprisals are lies," Chief Barton asserted, his face turning red. "Lies in your newspaper down here. We are a peaceful people. Always we have been friendly and helpful to you white people, particularly since the majority of us denounced the ways of old and adopted the ways of Christianity. We rely now on peaceful discussions in our village councils."

"What Chief Barton is saying is true, Gentlemen," Dr. Powell tried to reason with his Provincial Government counterparts. "I've seen the changes in Fort Simpson with my own eyes. Everything is decided by discussion in the Village Council. These chiefs have destroyed their longhouses of the past, done away with their Indian dances, and chopped and burned their pagen totems during Christian religious revivals at Reverend Crosby's direction. I assure you, if you were to visit Fort Simpson, you would view people living in a subdivision similar to the ones here in Victoria. Metlatakla was even more modern. Electricity was wired into every house there, although now I understand the generator has been removed to New Metlatakla in Alaska."

"The Premier and his Attorney-General gave a hoot of derision."

"I understand your loyalty to these Chiefs, Dr. Powell, in your capacity as Indian Commissioner under the Indian Act, but surely you can't expect us to believe that these Indians have the capacity to make wise decisions for themselves. It's the missionaries that should have the credit for these people turning against their pagan ways."

"Our ancestors were in a lose/lose, situation," I remarked to Rachel.

"Convert, adopt white ways and you lose your lands anyway. Resist and the English navy will deal with you."

"Now Chief Barton, we don't have all night, tell me, what are your demands? It's very important to me to end these tales of Indian threats and reprisals coming down from the North Coast. People in Victoria and on the mainland are very disturbed by them."

"How is it that you white people claim title to our lands, anyway?" Chief Barton demanded. "It makes no sense. We have never been conquered. We have never surrendered title. We have never signed treaties. We have never sold our land. We demand self-government of our villages and recognition of title for our land."

Premier Smithe went red with rage.

"Title to the land! See what I mean, Gentlemen. Self-government!" He looked at the whites in the room. "How could savages like these understand complicated concepts like private ownership of land and self-government? I'm telling you gentlemen, those Methodist missionaries we allowed to go amongst these people have done irreparable harm. They have filled these simple people's heads with big words and ridiculous demands."

Smithe rose to his feet and thundered at the Chiefs.

"Don't you people understand that you were no better than the wild beasts of the fields when the white people came among you? How could you have even have grasped a concept as complicated as private ownership of land."

"Premier Smithe," Dr. Powell interrupted. "Surely you will allow these Chiefs to expand on what they mean by self-government. I assure you, if you could view one of their village council meetings you would understand what they are saying."

"That will be enough Dr. Powell," Smithe silenced the Indian Commissioner." He seemed to make a heroic effort to calm down.

"Do you people have any more demands?" he asked sarcastically.

"We wish a public enquiry," Chief Barton responded. "To investigate how it came about that we no longer own our land. We want treaties made if the whites insist on pre-empting our land and coming amongst us. If we must suffer reserves they must be adequate, enough quality land that we might be self-sufficient. And guarantees of access to our fishing and hunting sites. And above all, we do not want an Indian Agent telling us what to do."

Smithe, his Attorney General and Land Commissioner looked at Chief Barton in complete disbelief.

"Perhaps a public enquiry?" suggested Indian Commissioner Powell diplomatically. "If you are sincere about wishing to end the threat of an Indian war?"

"Now you people listen to me," Smithe ignored Dr. Powell's suggestion. "You must get it through your simple heads that the Queen owns all the lands in Canada, including the lands of British Columbia. She makes the white people purchase the land. But because Indians are so far behind the white people, like children compared to the white man, the Queen is merciful to you. She puts land aside for reserves for her Indian children, until they can grow and become more like the white people."

The chiefs became visibly angry when Chief Barton translated Smithe's words.

"I suppose we could send some commissioners to Fort Simpson, Premier Smithe," the Attorney General interrupted, noticing their anger.

"For a public hearing. If these Chiefs will agree to end the disruption up there. I'm sure some arrangements can be made. I know just the gentlemen to send, Clement Cornwall and Joseph Plante." He winked knowingly at Premier Smithe. Smithe nodded understandingly.

"Why not?" he stated. "Well, Chief Barton? It's a damnable expense that the members of the legislature are not going to be thrilled about but I suppose if this will end the threat of hostilities."

Chief Barton conferred with the chiefs for several minutes. They looked unhappy but gave Chief Barton a nod."

"Very good, then," Smithe dismissed the Chiefs as if they were little boys. Dr. Powell led them out the door and back to their canoes. Premier Smithe and his officials left to return to the legislature.

"A lot of good that public inquiry did," Martha McBay snorted.

"What came of it, Darling," Nigel inquired.

"A few acres were added onto the reservations at Fort Simpson," Martha McBay commented. "And the Northwest Coast Indian Agency was established to govern from Bella Bella to the Nass Valley. Premier Smithe gave the Tsimshian people Indian Agents, police and Anglican missionaries to replace the rebellious William Duncan. This meant that the Heiltsuk, Nuxalt, Haisla, Haida, Tsimshian and Nishga'a people all came under the command and direction of an Indian Agent for the next sixty-four years."

"So much for recognition of Aboriginal Title and self-government," I commented.

"Didn't the Chiefs try and do anything to protest?" Rachel asked.

"Indeed they did," Martha McBay responded. "They continued to protest as even more good land was taken our of their existing reserves by O'Reilly all over British Columbia. For pre-emption by whites. Finally in 1912 a Joint Federal Provincial Commission, the McKenna-McBride Commission was convened to whitewash the legislated oppression of and marginalization of Indian people in British Columbia."

"What happened from that Commission, Gran?" All of a sudden Premier Smithe's parlor started to revolve.

"Make Raven stop, Gran," Rachel cried, as we were thrown to the floor with the speed of the revolutions.

"There's something else Raven wants you to see," Martha McBay answered.

I gasped as I could feel myself whirling through some kind of time vortex again.

When the disturbance stopped, I realised I was slumped over in a chair in someone's office. A tall, thin fellow in a navy blue suit was sitting behind a desk talking to a distinguished looking man with white hair. I glanced behind me. Rachel, Martha McBay and Nigel Kent were pulling themselves up from the floor. We were all now dressed in clothes appropriate for the nineteen twenties.

"Have a seat, Martha," I got up and helped Rachel's grandmother to sit down.

"Where are we now, Gran?" Rachel asked.

"That's the Premier of British Columbia in 1927, Dear, behind the desk. The Honorable John Oliver. And if I'm not mistaken, that other man is Duncan Campbell Scott, the Deputy Superintendent General of Indian Affairs. He was also a poet, of all things, and dedicated to the removal of the Indian problem through all-out policies of Assimilation."

We concentrated on their conversations.

"We've finally got the legislation you wanted in place, Mr. Premier. Legislation that should force the Natives in your Province to realise that their only hope for survival is to assimilate with the rest of us," Scott announced. He was beaming from ear to ear.

"I should hope so," the Premier of British Columbia advised. "You were present when Andrew Paull and Peter Kelly presented the Allied Tribes of B. C.'s comprehensive claim to aboriginal title to the special Senate-House Committee on the 8th. of March, of this year, Scott? What an outrage!"

"Yes, of course, Mister Premier. But you don't have to pay any attention to that claim now."

"The nerve of those natives. Of course it's all that Anglican Minister's fault, you know, Arthur O'meara. He's the only white still putting words in the native's mouths. Why, the claim they've put forth would negate everything that was decided by the McKenna-McBride Commission Report, after four years of public hearings and Peter O'Reilly, personally going over every square inch of reserve land in this Province."

"I know," Scott replied. "The land claim accuses us of ignoring the Aboriginal Title question, cutting off 47,000 acres of valuable land from the reserves, ignoring inequalities between Tribal groups and failing to address water rights and fisheries."

"All of which we did, of course," John Oliver chuckled. "But you say you've found a final solution to these legal claims problems."

"Yes, Mr. Premier. Once the Federal politicians realised that the Indians had discovered that the Royal Proclamation of 1763 guaranteed Aboriginal Title unless treaties extinguished it, they knew we had to act quickly. Imagine, the Allied Tribes were trying to petition the Privy Council in England on those grounds. But we've found a way to stop them in their tracks completely."

"How?" Oliver demanded.

"The 1927 Amendment to the Indian Act," Mr. Premier. Just passed by special order of the legislature. Section 141 of the statutes."

"How does it read, Scott?" The Deputy Superintendent pulled a sheet of paper out of his briefcase.

"Every person, who, without the consent of the Superintendent General expressed in writing, receives, obtains, solicits, or requests from any Indian any payment or contribution or promise of any payment or contribution for the purpose of raising a fund or providing money for the prosecution of any claim which the tribe or band of Indians to which such Indian belongs, or of which he is a member, has or is represented to have for the recovery of any claim or money for the benefit of the same tribe, shall be guilty of an offence and liable upon summary conviction for each such offence to a penalty not exceeding $200 and not less than $50 or to imprisonment for any term not exceeding two months."

"Excellent, Scott," Premier Oliver chuckled. "That should put those traitors like O'meara out of action, for sure. They need your written permission to pursue a claim, particularly a land claim, do they? I presume you're be giving permission for that?"

"You know how much I'm absolutely committed to Assimilation, Mr. Premier."

"Have a cigar, Scott. We need to celebrate. A brandy in the House lounge?"

"That's the companion legislation to the Potlatch Prohibition," Martha McBay snorted us as the two, happy bureaucrats marched off arm-in-arm.

"With that legislation, our people were forbidden to hold a potlatch or act in any capacity on a land claim from 1927 to 1951. We were also stuck with the loss of 47,000 acres of desirable land from the reserves. Our children were hauled off to Residential Schools, white-owned canneries were allotted our fishing and water rights by the Federal Government, our grazing lands for our cattle were taken back, and white entrepreneurs were granted timber rights and mineral rights from the lands we had never sold or surrendered. White settlers and land speculators were allowed to pre-empt the remainder of our lands all over this Province."

"But we survived, Gran," Rachel said.

"Not too well, Dear. I'm sure Raven is going to show us some present conditions on many of our reserves."

"And our culture is being brought back, Gran."

"That's certainly reason for celebration," Martha McBay's voice echoed as a whirling vortex seized us again. I relaxed this time and tried not to fight the vortex. When my dizziness stopped, I realized that Rachel and I were back sitting on a log at Chemainus. In front of the five dugouts that would follow Clarissa across the Strait of Georgia to mainland B. C. again.

"I can't take much more of this, Paul," Rachel gasped as we gained consciousness. I looked for Martha McBay and Nigel and sighed as they were in sight still loading things into the canoes.

"Face it, Rachel," I ventured. "The Potlatch Legislation, the ban on land claim activity, and the Indian Residential Schools were done deliberately to force Assimilation. Not to mention "Enfranchisement."

"Enfranchisement?"

"Removal from the band lists, Rachel. With or without permission. For going to the city. For attending College or University. To claim the low-interest housing loans returned veterans were entitled to you had to accept enfranchisement. If you were a woman and married a non-native, you and your children were enfranchised. That meant if your marriage failed and you returned to your community neither you or your children were eligible for band-sponsored housing."

"That must have caused endless suffering, Paul."

"It did, Rachel. So much so that mothers denied status even occupied Indian Affairs offices in Vancouver. And their counterparts in New Brunswick staged a women's march to Ottawa."

"It was the United Nations that forced a change in the status legislation for women, wasn't it Paul?"

"That's correct. They ruled against Canada when Sandra Lovelace put in a legal complaint to the Human Discriminations court at the Hague."

"I remember. That was in 1985."

"See how effective protest is, Rachel. Become an activist like me," I advised her. "The two of us would make a great pair."

"Activism is a little out of my line, Paul," Rachel answered with a wan smile."

"You never know, Rachel. After all, I don't imagine Raven is through with us yet."

We made our way over to the canoes.

"We're changing the route," I advised all the paddlers after Martha McBay had led us in the cleansing ritual. "We're going to hug the mainland of B. C. instead of going up the protected east coast of Vancouver Island. As far as Quadra Island, anyway, I thought, remembering Clarissa's secret directions.

The paddlers looked at me in shock.

"We'll make it to Bella Bella, for sure," I promised the paddlers. "For Nate and the generations to follow us. Nate would have wanted us to finish this journey."

Rachel and the others nodded sadly.

Once I was in the canoe I allowed myself to dwell on the information I was not sharing with the others.

Clarissa's words haunted me as I matched Martha's McBay's rhythmic drumming with paddle strokes.

"Don't tell the others, Paul but it may not be just some isolated lunatic we are dealing with in these attacks."

"The R. C. M. P. have found out something?"

"They are keeping an eye on a Newslist on the Internet, Paul. Unfortunately the reporting on Nate Archer's murder gave all kinds of publicity that we didn't need to the "Voyage of Solidarity." Most people are extremely sympathetic but the R.C.M.P tell me that some of the right wing extremists in this province were disappointed that the journey wasn't stopped in its tracks by the attack and the murder. One of them started one of those newslists on the Internet and attracted quite a few of the resident loonies. There's some group dedicating themselves to finishing what our other attacker started. The police say that there's more than two hundred members subscribed to the list."

"You don't suppose any of them own boats of some sort, do you? Boats that could be used to interfere with our dugouts."

"There's no way of telling, Paul. The R. C. M. P. say that some of these groups are all talk but they are monitoring the newslist and any e-mail amongst it's members. We're going to have to keep all traces of our route and timelines for arrival from public knowledge."

"Well, we already know we've got one person, at least, willing to stop at nothing to prevent us from reaching Bella Bella. But you know, Clarissa, all someone has to do is to keep a eye on both routes up to Bella Bella. The inner passage one and the one along the mainland. Sooner or later someone is going to spot our group of canoes."

"I know, Paul. I'm trying to organize more escort vessels. At the present time if more than one boat attacks at once, the paddler's are in great danger."

"We need communication devices, Clarissa. In each canoe and in your boat."

"I'll take care of that, immediately, Paul. Good idea."

CHAPTER 10

Intimidation By Air

It was another spectacularly beautiful day as the dugouts left Chemainus and set off for a paddle to the Gulf Islands of British Columbia. Clarissa had decided to throw their attacker off the scent by switching the route from the sheltered coast off Vancouver Island's east coast where the canoes could work their way from sheltered beach to sheltered beach to the much more demanding coast off the mainland of British Columbia.

"Follow my trawler," she had ordered Paul Archer. "I'm going to divert through Pender Island up to Galiano Island and then over to Tsawwassen on the mainland. Whoever made that attack ten days ago will be watching for us somewhere north of here to try another assault. Let's hope he doesn't catch on that we've altered course."

Rachel felt her body strained to the fullest as she tried to keep up with the pace of the other paddlers in the Heiltsuk canoe. Her bruised and battered tissue had still not healed completely. By the time the tip of South Pender Island came into view around noon every bone, joint and muscle in the right side of her body was protesting furiously.

"We'll stop for lunch in one of those little coves," Paul decided, taking in the pain on Rachel's face.

"These islands are magical, Dear," Rachel looked up at her grandmother's voice as the older women sat down beside her on one of the logs that had drifted in to the little cove.

"I just love the Garry Oaks and Arbutus trees set on every rock and cranny of these islands," Gran added. Rachel glanced out at the gorgeous scenery around them. The red and brown Arbutus trees were particularly colourful. Light blue and green water glistened against the white sands, grey slate, and coloured pebbles of the beaches sprinkled with broken and ground up white, oyster and clam shells.

Small crabs and shell-fish of all kinds chased after each other in the tide-pools. Large, barnacle-covered rocks sat like nature-carved statues on the shores. Behind them, architecturally-designed cedar post and beam vacation homes peeking through the still surprisingly forested green plateaus where the cliffs allowed occupation testified to the popularity of the Gulf Islands. They were a chain of volcanic islands set in the ocean between Vancouver Island and the coast of British Columbia directly above the San Juan Islands of Washington State.

"I'm even beginning to forget to smell the roses," Rachel admonished herself as the food and the rest break seemed to placate her complaining body.

"You're right, Gran," she smiled at her only remaining relative, marvelling at her never-failing enthusiasm for life's experiences. "These islands do have something special about them."

A flock of light-brown sea-gulls suddenly started calling out to each other and dive-bombing the ocean just off the shore.

"Look, they're dive bombing two seals," Gran laughed. "They must think the seals are stealing their herring."

Rachel focused on the raucous scene. "You're right Gran," she laughed. "Every time one of those seals comes to the surface for air those sea gulls dive-bomb it. I swear the seals are teasing the gulls."

A little optimism flowed back into Rachel's mind.

"There seems to be all kinds of wild life here," she added, staring at cormorants sitting on rocks in the distance, and the eagles and hawks swirling in circles far above them. "Pollution can't be as bad as I had supposed."

"These islands are full of wild deer and pheasants as well," Paul joined in the conversation.

"By the time the canoes pushed off again, on a course for the tip of North Pender Island to stay the night, Rachel hardly noticed the stiffness in her bones.

"That prescription for inflammation I had from the doctor has really helped," she thought. "Thank God I brought it along."

"That's Beaumont Marine Park, " Paul Archer told her as they passed an absolutely gorgeous stretch of beach with a peninsula jutting out complete with a small white and red lighthouse. Picnic tables and platforms for tents could be seen next to the shoreline.

"The only way that campsite can be reached is by water or by hiking in," Paul advised.

"A little further up the island we'll come to a spit of land. It's the entrance to Browning Harbor. There was an architectural dig on the spit some years back and the archeologists found evidence of First Nations' presence dating back over five thousand years in the midden they explored."

"Oh, My God," Rachel exclaimed, interrupting Paul's lecture about the Penders.

"What's the matter?" Paul demanded.

"That plane coming towards us, isn't it unusually low?" Rachel pointed to a small green and white plane in the distance heading directly towards them at full speed. It seemed to be flying awfully close to the water.

"Oh, don't worry," Paul advised. "Float planes are always landing and taking off around these islands."

"That's not a float plane, Paul," Nigel advised. "It's a Cessna, if I'm not mistaken."

"Probably just some tourist," Paul commented. "Out for a joy ride. Probably wants a photograph of the canoes at close range or something."

"Close is right," Nigel added. "That plane can't be fifty feet above the water."

The sound of Clarissa's boat motor picked up as she moved closer to the lead canoe.

"She's spotted the plane, too."

Clarissa moved her boat directly in the front of their canoe.

"What the Hell is going on?" Paul became alarmed as well as Rachel.

"I've got a funny feeling about that plane," Gran warned as the Cessna continued its approach.

"It's going to crash into the poles of Clarissa's trawler if it doesn't gain some altitude fast." The plane's motor was getting deafening as the small craft kept on it's interception course. It seemed to be losing even more altitude.

As it approached Clarissa's boat the nose of the plane suddenly went up, and a blast of motor noise alerted the canoeists that the plane was going to pass over them. It went by with a blast of air striking the paddlers.

"The crazy fool," Nigel stated. "Did anyone get his registration number. We should report him to the authorities."

"The number on the wing was covered over," Rachel warned.

"Mother Jesus," Nigel swore.

"It's coming back for another pass," Paul shouted. "Be prepared to jump!"

A bang from Clarissa's fishboat alerted them that she was firing towards the plane with some kind of pistol.

"That's a flare gun," Paul told them. Within seconds a bright red flare lit up in the sky in front of the plane.

"Damn, he's not turning back," Nigel yelled.

Another bang came from the flare gun and another red flash near the plane lit up the sky.

"That's no tourist," Paul yelled. "Too bad Clarissa used the flare gun. She should have used the elephant gun." He waved his arms, motioning for the canoes to disburse. They responded instantly moving off in different directions.

The plane dove strait down towards Clarissa. Her boat remained slightly ahead of the canoe Rachel was in but directly in front like a mother hen trying to protect it's young.

The plane suddenly veered away from Clarissa's boat.

"It's going for one of the other canoes," Paul decided. "There's nothing we can do."

Clarissa spotted the manoeuvre and her boat suddenly shot to the left ahead of them and picked up it's speed. Clarissa agonizingly turned the boat around and moved back past the lead canoe towards the threatened canoe. But she was too late.

The Cessna was already upon the Nuu'chah‚nulth canoe, approaching it in a fast dive.

Rachel could see the paddlers in the Nuu'chah'nulth canoe ducking down and placing their hands over their heads as the Cessna came roaring down at them. She braced herself for a crash.

At the last minute the plane pulled it's nose up. Rachel gasped. Something had been thrown out the open door of the Cessna as it roared upwards just a few feet above the canoe. Something white was scattering everywhere.

"Leaflets," Nigel shouted.

A sudden huge explosion filled the air.

"Clarissa's trying to knock that thing out of the sky with the elephant gun," Paul's voice shouted approval.

As Rachel watched the Cessna pulled higher in the air and kept flying straight ahead.

"I guess he's not going to take any further chances with that gun," Nigel shouted.

"Too bad Clarissa missed!"

Rachel could hear huge sighs of relief all around her in the Heiltsuk canoe as the plane kept flying away from them and finally disappeared into the distance.

"Not very brave, are they?"

Clarissa's motor noise went down as she slowly moved towards the Nuu'chah'nulth canoe.

"Paddle over," Paul yelled. All the canoes headed in the same direction.

Clarissa's trawler got there first. By the time Paul's canoe paddled over, the Nuu'chah'nulth canoeists were staring in horror at some of the white sheets of paper that the plane had dropped. Clarissa was on deck with one of the leaflets in her hand.

"What does it say?" Paul shouted. He scooped up one of the wet sheets from the water. Rachel looked over his shoulder. "END THIS VOYAGE OR NEXT TIME IT WON'T BE PAPER!" she read. Rachel went into shock as she realised that the "Voyage of Solidarity" had more enemies than just some lone maniac with an old fishboat.

Rachel felt a horrible nausea hit her in the pit of her stomach.

"We've picked up some more resident crazies," Paul commented as he processed what he was reading.

"Let's hope they're not as whacko as Nate Archer's murderer," Nigel said, his voice betraying the fury he was feeling.

"Keep on towards North Pender," Clarissa shouted. "We don't want to let those terrorists think they've succeeded," she added.

Paul Archer nodded his head in agreement. Everybody in all the canoes gave a cheer.

"To the tip of North Pender," Paul shouted, lowering his paddle into the water. The others followed his example and within three hours the dugouts had made it to Clam Bay on North Pender Island, their destination for the night.

"There's no way we're going to be able to keep the route secret," Paul complained to Clarissa as they were discussing what to do about the latest development.

"And we don't know whether those people in the plane were just trying to intimidate us or if they really do intend to drop something on our heads a lot more dangerous than leaflets."

"We'll go up the coast off the mainland, anyway," Clarissa sighed. "There's not as much air traffic that way once we're past Vancouver. I'll radio ahead to our friends from the Tsawwassen, Squamish or Musqueam bands. Maybe one of their members is an amateur pilot or something. Looks like we need air cover as well as an escort vehicle."

"Too bad be can't get our hands on one of those ground-to-air light missiles soldiers carry on their backs," Paul advised, angrily. "Like they used in Afghanistan. That would do the trick."

"That's a good suggestion, Paul. I thought you were non-violent?"

"I'm rapidly losing my convictions," Paul confessed.

CHAPTER 11

Martha McBay

Three more dugout canoes joined the voyageurs as they stopped over at a remote beach on Galiano Island for three days after their intimidation by air. The new dugouts had been scheduled to rendezvous as the original canoes made their way up the east coast of Vancouver Island but Clarissa had given new directions to their Canoe Societies when they left Chemainus.

The dugout canoe, of the Comox Nation, the "I-hos," or in English, "Sea Serpent," met up with the others first. It was a canoe left natural except for black paint around it's designs. The dugout canoe of the Weiwaikum Nation of Campbell River, named "Lightning Speed" turned up the next day just before nightfall. The "Lightning Speed," from Campbell River, had "Thunderbird" painted on it's side. The third day, the Namgis Nation canoe, the "Galuda" from Alert Bay paddled into the new rendezvous site.

Martha McBay stared at the dugout from Alert Bay with particular admiration. It had a carved wooden loon on it's bow complete with wooden wings that could be manouvered to lift up and down. It made quite an impression on anyone watching from the shore.

All the paddlers took part in a "Pow Wow" around the "sacred fire" on the remote Galiano beach.

"The 'ancestors' must be pleased," Martha McBay mused. "Imagine, all these dugout canoes have been carved recently by First Nations' people on Vancouver Island and the lower coast of B. C., except for the Heiltsuk canoe, of course. What a resurgence of culture. And all of these newly initiated 'Secret Canoe Societies' warriors that refuse to be intimidated. Imagine, not one paddler has decided to turn back, even with Nate Archer's death, the attack at Chemainus and the warning from that Cessna." Martha could feel powerful vibrations around the 'sacred fire.'

The next morning the paddlers of the eight canoes joined in the morning cleansing ceremonies and then moved off to paddle across the open waters of Georgia Strait to Tsawwassen. It took over seventeen hours for all of them to reach a beach near Tsawwassen on the mainland.

Paul took advantage of darkness to move the canoes through Vancouver Harbor. He even used running lights to avoid collision. Clarissa did not want any surprise photos of the canoes in the Vancouver newspapers alerting their original attacker, at the very least, to the change in route.

Martha gasped as she realized how small the dugouts were compared to the giant ocean-going freighters they passed anchored out in Vancouver's Harbor.

"And our ancestors really used these vessels to trade along the coast all the way from Alaska to the Washington and Oregon coasts," she thought.

It took two weeks to slowly work their way up the B. C. Coast past Texada Island and Powell River. The paddlers camped in secret in solitary coves and beaches they found on the way utilizing tents and packing their own provisions. There were no more attacks by air much to Clarissa's disappointment. She had somehow managed to locate one of the prohibited ground-to-air missiles and kept it in a handy spot in the wheelhouse.

As they reached Cape Mudge on Quadra Island the paddlers of the Fort Rupert canoe, the "Maxwalogwa," joined the other eight vessels. Then the nine canoes took over several days of heavy duty paddling to reach the waters of the Homalco people on the mainland of British Columbia at the mouth of Bute Inlet.

Martha McBay stared in awe at the sharply plunging cliffs above Bute Inlet at Churchhouse. It was the location of the almost abandoned reserve of the Homalco people, where the paddlers would be spending the weekend. She couldn't believe the changes in scenery the paddlers had experienced on their journey. The low bank waterfront off of the west coast of Vancouver Island had transformed into the beauty of the Gulf Islands. Then they had all paddled by the rather stark cliffs overlooking the cold waters off Squamish and the Sunshine Coast. Now they were viewing the extremely scenic but demanding waters of the upper mainland coast. The deep fiords of the river inlets from the sea with their sharply plunging cliffs took her breath away.

The time had passed without any further threatening incidences.

"Those fellows in the plane must have been just trying to frighten us," Martha mused. "But I wonder what's happened to Nate Archer's murderer in the white and grey fishboat. He must have been confused because of our change in route."

The exertion necessary to paddle through the dangerous waters along the Vancouver west coast, and beyond Quadra Island was taking it's toll on everyone. Paul Archer had decided they needed a weekend free of paddling to recuperate. It was a decision that had been particularly welcomed by Martha McBay. Her heart and her head were still reeling from Nigel Kent's proposition that he had put to her just before the canoes had left Quadra Island.

Nigel had given her his usual friendly hug around her shoulders as they were staring alone at the still brightly burning campfire on the beach at the tip of Quadra Island. He had been showing her his most recent drawings for Rachel's book.

Tears had come to Martha's eyes at the power in Nigel's drawings. The disbelief, fear and terror in the little residential school student's eyes as she cowered at the vicious slap administered by the Mother Superior was only too realistic. Martha gasped as she stared at Nigel's portrait of the tiny student being sexually molested by the drunken priest. The pain and self-loathing in the child's eyes brought intense, repressed feelings of her own sexual abuse into Martha's mind.

Martha winced as she stared at a recent portrait of a man lying in a passive position next to a canoe on one of the beaches they had landed on. His expression was of deep pain and depression. Nigel had done a good job disguising the man's features, but Martha realised he had to be one of the slightly older paddlers in one of the Canoe Societies' dugouts. He had been sent to paddle the journey by one of the Native Counsellors in his Tribal Council as a last resort to lessen his chronic depression.

It was Alphonse Jack. His eyes in the portrait said it all. They reflected his sense of hopelessness about the future. Alphonse had confided his problems to Martha. She knew of his low self-worth, his inability to form lasting relationships with the opposite sex, his inability to even get out of bed for days on end, his sense of victimization, his inability to find and keep any kind of employment, and his frequent alteration from deep depression to dangerous anger outbursts under the influence of alcohol. Martha knew he had been one of the last students at the Alberni Indian Residential School.

"I didn't think any white person could understood, Nigel," she gasped. "The pain of our people. The years of hopelessness, the feelings of victimization and not being able to cope with life, the refusal to give up the fight against innumerable odds, and the hope that somehow things would be better for future generations of First Nations' children."

Her voice had been silenced as Nigel had pulled her against him and kissed her tenderly on the mouth.

Martha recalled her surprise at the intensity of the warmth and love coming at her from Nigel. She could feel his love thawing the coldness and feeling of severe loneliness around her own heart. She found herself responding passionately to Nigel's tentative embrace. Her response encouraged Nigel further and within ten minutes the two of them found themselves making passionate love under Nigel's double sleeping bag in his tent.

"I had no idea you were interested in anything more than my mind, Dear," Martha had gasped when both of them had satisfied what Martha had considered were her long dead passions of the flesh.

"I didn't think those parts even worked any more."

She and Nigel were clinging to each other tenderly on Nigel's air mattress.

"I love you, Martha," Nigel confessed. "With all my heart, Darling. It happened almost immediately when I first met you, but I was afraid that you would have nothing to do with one of the members of the very nationality that had oppressed and marginalized your people."

Tears came to Martha McBay's eyes. She patted Nigel's hand lightly. From the poignancy in his voice she realised that Nigel had been loving her from a distance for much of the canoe journey.

"You were right to wait, Dear," she told him. "I most assuredly would not have been open to the overtures of an eccentric film director from England. Particularly one who was ordering me into a series of uncomfortable positions in a cramped and tippy dugout canoe so he could get the right camera angle."

"Eccentric film director?" Nigel looked taken aback.

"Delightfully so, Dear," Martha reassured him.

"And very talented. Your drawings of the Hamatsa, and the Mother Superior looming over that poor student as well as the priest sexually molesting the little girl in the infirmary will strike terror into the hearts of the readers of Rachel's book."

"Thank you, Darling," Nigel picked up her right hand and kissed it tenderly.

Martha watched in amazement as Nigel got up out of the sleeping bag and rummaged around in one of his canvas dufflebags.

"He looks Damn good in those boxer shorts," Martha said to herself as she surveyed Nigel in the brightness of a propane light. She gasped as she realised what he was pulling out of the dufflebag. Nigel had a small, wooden, jewelry box in his hand.

"Martha, I won't expect an answer tonight," he informed her. "But I want you to accompany me to French Tahiti. I've received an offer to do a documentary about the Sovereignty movement in Tahiti. I want you to come with me as my wife."

Martha gasped as tears flooded into her eyes. Nigel sat down on the edge of the precarious cot and placed an engagement ring on her finger.

"That's so beautiful, Nigel." Martha stared at the ring in amazement. It had a Haida design in the gold ring. It's claws were enclosing a green emerald.

"It's a "Bill Reid" original," Nigel explained. "A friend of mine picked it up for me in Vancouver."

Martha stared at the English film director in disbelief. She realised he was completely infatuated with her. She could feel the warmth in his heart and his fear that she would reject him radiating into her own heart. The depth of Nigel's love touched something deep within Martha. She made up her mind on the spot.

"I'll marry you, Nigel," Martha felt herself promising despite the reasons she shouldn't flooding into her consciousness.

"For better or worse?" he asked. "Until death do us part?"

"You drive a hard bargain, Dear," Martha told him. She nodded and felt a slight, rueful smile come to her face.

"I don't know how I'm going to explain this to Rachel," she complained. Nigel gathered her tenderly in his arms.

"Wait till we get to Bella Bella, Darling," Nigel advised her. "Rachel is having a big enough growth period as it is."

Martha McBay returned to the present with a start as the canoes got within sight of the long pier jutting out in front of the old, white church at Churchhouse. She reached for and touched her hand on Nigel's exquisite engagement ring. Martha was wearing it on a gold chain next to her heart under her wool sweater.

Martha forced herself to concentrate on the present. A number of boats were dropping off a collection of First Nations People of all ages onto the dock. As the people on the dock and on shore caught sight of the flotilla of ceremonial canoes they broke into a shout of welcome.

"How wonderful," an elder greeted the paddlers in the first

canoe as it moved into the dock behind an outgoing fishboat. "Welcome to Aupe Reserve No. 6 at Churchhouse. We had no idea the dugouts had reached this far."

"What's going on?" Paul Archer inquired. "We were told that this reserve is all but abandoned."

"You're just in time for a Homalco retreat and Community Sharing Circle," the elder told Paul. "We would be honoured if you would join us for the ceremonies. What you are doing for the First Nations's people of British Columbia is nothing short of sacred," he told them.

Hordes of excited people came running down the old pier and helped the paddlers unload their gear as the other canoes and Clarissa's fishboat pulled into the dock.

"What's a Community Sharing Circle, Gran?" Rachel asked her as the paddlers were getting their tents and sleeping bags ready for the night. The group readily agreed to take part in the Circle as they were staying for a rest break that weekend anyway.

"It's a meeting of the whole community, Dear," Martha told her grand-daughter. "Usually a serious problem has surfaced. It's a traditional approach to confront the problem or problems and brainstorm answers for their solution."

"Won't we be intruding?" Paul Archer asked.

"I think you will find that the problems the Homalco people are experiencing aren't that different from the ones that Heiltsuk or Haida people are experiencing, Dear," Martha replied.

"I'm going to ask permission to video at least some of the ceremony," Nigel rushed off.

"He's so enthusiastic about life," Martha sighed. She realised that as long as Nigel was alive things would never seem boring again.

Promptly at 7:00 p.m., most of the paddlers joined with the Homalco people on the lawn beside the old, white church. An Homalco elder lit the "Sacred Fire" and the majority of people from the Homalco reserve on Vancouver Island as well as paddlers from the First Nations' Canoe Societies, and the few people left in the Churchhouse reserve all danced around it to the beat of drumming.

An Homalco elder conducted the "Pipe Ceremony" and all present passed around the "Pipe."

"The smoke from the pipe connects all of us with 'Great Spirit.' 'Great Mystery,' and the 'Ancestors,' Martha McBay told Rachel and Paul Archer.

The Homalco elder gave a speech about the need for a return to the traditional principles of balance, harmony, and order. He spoke about the need to restore a sense of connectiveness to the land.

The elder informed the group that there would be an opportunity for those that wished to take part in a river bathing purification with cedar boughs. A cheer went up from the crowd.

The ceremonial singing and drumming around the 'Sacred Fire' went on for several hours. In the morning, after a communal breakfast, the over two hundred participants were divided into ten small groups to discuss relevant questions affecting the community. Rachel, and Gran found themselves in the group that were instructed to discuss urban First Nations' problems and brainstorm solutions to them.

Their group was meeting in one part of the old church. Martha McBay sat down next to one of the middle-aged women from the Vancouver Island, Homalco group.

"Hi, I'm Florence Joseph," the woman introduced herself. "I can't believe how this village has changed since I lived here in the nineteen forties and fifties," she said. "This place is almost like a ghost town now."

"Why did everyone leave?" Martha asked.

Florence Joseph recounted the changes that caused the Homalco people to leave Churchhouse. Martha noted that Rachel was listening intently. She nodded approvingly.

Florence told them that it was because her father and others could no longer make a living. She explained what it was like growing up here in Christchurch. Florence recounted how her father did all right in the thirties and early forties. She told them how he had salvaged logs from the coastline and fished for the canneries in the summer.

"But then," Florence's voice had sorrow in it, "the timber harvesting rights were given exclusively to the big logging companies that sprouted up after the war and the fishing licenses were given to the large commercial fishboats.

We were forbidden to pick up salvage logs. The big companies hired a company from the Coast to salvage the logs. Even if we wanted the logs to saw up for lumber for ourselves we had to purchase the logs from the company. Without fishing and logging my father and other Homalco people couldn't survive here. The same thing happened all along the coast. Most of us went to the cities in search of work. Either Vancouver or Victoria."

"Same thing in Bella Bella," Martha said sadly. Things got even worse just lately in 1991 when the Federal Government's solution to the dwindling of the salmon stocks was to halve the number of fishing licenses. That's put many Heiltsuk on the welfare roles."

"It's the same on the Queen Charlottes," Paul said. "Most of the proud fishing boats in Masset and Skidegate are sitting idle, waiting for the banks to repossess them."

"What precipitated this "Sharing Circle?" Rachel asked.

"Suicide," Florence told them. "Another of our teenagers killed himself. We've had an epidemic of this kind of thing on Vancouver Island."

"That's so sad," Martha heard her grand-daughter comment.

"We had the same problem in Bella Bella, Dear, some years back," Martha found herself reminding Rachel. "Remember when they sent that "Crisis Intervention Team," up from the Coast a decade ago. Why, it had gotten so bad that the main topic of conversation in the Elementary school was funerals. Students were even bringing in undertaker catalogs to make choices of options in burials."

"I remember seeing those flyers, Gran," Rachel answered. She looked quite distraught. "No wonder you gave permission for me to be boarded down in Vancouver for High School so quickly."

"The Land Claims are our only hope for our young people," Florence Joseph remarked.

"Why do you think that?" Rachel asked.

"If we can get some control of our own resources back like timber, fishing, and mining there would be jobs for people living on the reserves. If we manage to secure self-government and control of education, then our young people would be able to have hope of employment in a professional capacity after they attend the new post-secondary First Nations training institutions like the Nicola Valley one."

"As things are now the young people are forced to leave for the cities. Adjustment is hard down there. It's not the same as white people changing their location. Many of the white people have private property they can sell for money to purchase a new home. Our reserves are communal so when Native people go to the cities they can't retrieve any investment from land they own and have to pay high rents. Our children are not accustomed to the competition in the classrooms in the big cities. Teachers in the schools have little tolerance for kids that need more help than the average. And outright racism does linger on."

"I know," Gran commented. "By the time our people come back to us they have lost hope that the future will ever be any better. And there is never enough housing on the reserves."

"It's so unfair," Florence Joseph continued. The white government of the British settlers and the entrepreneurs and land developers that came with them made sure that we were stripped of every resource that the white's considered valuable."

"What did the Homalco people lose to the whites?" Rachel asked.

Martha McBay listened with satisfaction as Florence gave Rachel a lecture on what happened to the Homalco people. Florence told Rachel that they had almost lost Churchhouse, itself, when the reserves were being adjusted by Peter O'reilly. She recounted how a white school teacher, who had come to Churchhouse in 1909, had pre-empted the already cleared ground that the school, church, houses, garden sites and cemeteries of the Homalco people were on. The reserve lost five acres to the teacher. The only thing that had saved the village was that the school teacher's pre-emption had been reduced by the McBride-McKenna Commission.

"However, this reserve was reduced by nine acres, too," she testified, "when the B. C. government was not salified with the Commission recommendations and the Premier sent out two more civil servants to reassess the matter."

"And our people did not receive the fishing rights at the river mouths they assumed went with the land. Those were doled out by the Federal Government to white entrepreneurs and white cannery owners."

Martha McBay told them that the same thing happened at Bella Bella and to the Tsimshian and Nishga'a on the Nass and Skeena rivers. She told Rachel and Florence that after the McKenna-McBride Commission in 1916 the whole Nass Valley was opened for white pre-emption, mining and logging.

"As late as 1979, by a special order by the Federal Cabinet, the Amex mine was constructed without even a tailings ponds," Paul testified. "Just a pipe flushing the arsenic and other poisons from the metal extraction in the processing mills. The pipe ended fifty metres beneath the sea. No wonder the fish stocks declined."

The elder leading the group discussion about urban problems joined the circle and Martha McBay's thoughts came back to the present. The elder, Rachel and Paul Archer listened as one Homalco member told them of an innovative program that was happening in Winnipeg. A volunteer car patrol had been set up to respond to a crisis line operating out of one of the Native Friendship Centres there. The volunteer car patrol operated on Friday and Saturday nights in North End Winnipeg to respond to crises. The patrol cruised the streets and responded to fights outside bars and in alleys, to harassment of native women by Johns mistaking them for prostitutes, to intoxications and overdoses, and to petty crime, family violence and threats of suicide. They also ran unsupervised children home in their car, mediated conflicts and gave assistance to anyone who was intoxicated, self-destructive or in need of help.

"Sounds great," Paul remarked.

'Yes, but the patrol will likely have to stop," the elder complained. "There's no official funds for it's operation."

"That's because of "Enfranchisement," Martha McBay told Paul and Rachel afterwards.

"Enfranchisement," Rachel questioned. "That's what Paul was telling me about. In Chemainus, I think."

"Actually, it should have been called disenfranchisement. It was Deputy Superintendent Duncan Scott's fourth plank in legislation aimed at forcing Indians to assimilate with whites. In 1920 he passed another amendment to the Indian Act allowing natives who left their reserves to be taken off the Status Indian rolls, with or without their permission. They became so-called "enfranchised" to become full citizens of Canada and all monies due to their bands by status registration were lost. Indian women who married a non-status person or white person were also "enfranchised" as well as their offspring. Young people going to College or University were also "enfranchised," losing their status rights. Even Natives who had fought in World War II had to be enfranchised in order to claim the low-interest loans available to veterans for housing."

"That meant that Natives off the reserves had no special services or funding," Paul commented. "And that Native women and their children returning to the reserves if their marriages broke down had no guaranteed housing or rights."

"It's all so depressing," Rachel commented. "Thank Heavens you're around, Gran, to help me cope with it all."

Martha McBay felt a mixture of gladness that Rachel was finally understanding what had happened to her people and pain around her heart as she realised she was going to have to tell Rachel soon that she would be going away with Nigel.

Sunday morning there was a sharing of the consensus reached

in the small discussion groups with the full community sharing circle. A spokesperson from each group relayed their findings. Then Rachel, Paul and Martha McBay took part in a ritual purification session using cedar boughs to brush off any negativity in the cold water at Churchhouse. One of the Homalco elders guided them through traditional songs and rituals.

"I do feel a little better," Rachel confessed the next morning as the paddlers prepared to resume their taxing schedule.

"The singing of the traditional songs releases pain, sorrow and anger, Dear," Martha McBay told her grand-daughter, "and the rituals allow a release of emotion."

CHAPTER 12

Another Incident

Three weeks after leaving Churchhouse the paddlers were sensing victory. They had worked their way through the rough waters of Johnstone Strait and were into the Queen Charlotte Strait within two weeks of reaching Namu. Clarissa told them of the success of the four dugout canoes coming down the Coast to Bella Bella. Canoes from the Tsimshian people, the Haida Nation on the Queen Charlottes, the Kitimaaat Nation and the Bella Coola, Nuxult, Nation were getting closer to where all the dugouts would rendezvous and move in unison to Bella Bella.

Everyone in all the canoes were joyous at the news, even Alphonse Jack, who was observed smiling and laughing for the first time in many years. Rachel McBay was talking animatedly with Paul Archer as both of them paddled furiously along with their colleagues towards their night's rest at Seymour Inlet.

"Gran was absolutely right, Paul," Rachel felt enormous pain around her heart as she ruthlessly evaluated her last eight years. "I spent all this time in the white man's educational system, and never bothered to investigate my own people's cultural and healing traditions."

"Don't be so hard on yourself, Rachel," Paul told her. "You and I both have received quite an education on this canoe voyage. And your degrees are needed by our people. You'll see. You'll be snapped up fast by one of the First Nation's Mental Health service providers."

"I still have so much to learn, Paul. Thank God Gran is around to teach me."

"Don't be too sure about that Rachel, but don't worry. I'm more than willing to replace your grandmother for you," he volunteered. "I'll turn you into an activist yet. Tell you what, I'm going down to a conference in Oregon in September. All the warriors for Indigenous people's rights will be there. Why don't you join me?"

"What do you mean, Paul, about Gran, that is?"

"Haven't you noticed how close she and Nigel have become, Rachel?" Paul lowered his voice.

"Gran and Nigel?"

"They try and hide it, Rachel, but if you watch them closely the look they give each other every now and then, pretty intense, if you ask me. I think it's great, too bad they aren't younger."

Rachel thought about how many times Gran had been slow in coming to bed lately. "For some time," she realised. Rachel admitted to herself that Gran had got into the habit of talking to Nigel around the campfire.

"My God, Paul, you don't think they're going to go run off somewhere together, do you? At their age?"

"I think you should consider the possibility, Rachel," Paul warned.

Suddenly Rachel felt all alone, almost like she had been abandoned. She shivered suddenly, feeling extremely cold again. Paul gave her a warm hug.

"Think about coming with me to Oregon in September, Rachel," he urged. "That conference could be the start of a whole new way of life for us."

Rachel stared at Paul in surprise. She realised with a shock that he was quite serious. Rachel flushed beet red as she became uncomfortably aware of Paul's considerable attractiveness.

"Paul, I have to defend my Doctorate," she protested. "And I just want to learn more about Native Spirituality, not passive resistance methods."

"Native Spirituality and passive resistance methods are closely linked, Rachel." Paul advised. "Haven't you heard David Cardinal, the famous First Nations architect talking about "Soft Power.""

"Soft power?" Rachel blurted in astonishment.

"Caring and commitment, together, Rachel. I memorized Cardinal's and Jeannette Armstrong's words. From a book they wrote together. They said that "We know our lives to be the tools of the vast human dream mind which is continuing on into the future." And that "you need that centre (caring and commitment) to make a contribution creatively. You need to realize it's power to make it realize your vision. You have visions and dreaming but how you realize them depends on caring and commitment."

"That's very deep, Paul."

"Take time to think about it, Rachel. We still have two months until the conference."

That evening Rachel retired early from the campfire complaining of tiredness. Two hours later she woke up and noticed Gran was still not present. She left her tent and glanced over at the still-burning campfire. Nigel and Gran were the only ones left at it. Rachel started as they were in a very intimate embrace. She went back to her tent without disturbing them.

"Paul's right," Rachel realised. "About Gran and Nigel, anyway." Tears came to her eyes. A strange mixture of emotions were churning through her stomach. Both happiness for Gran and fear at losing her only relative and source of knowledge about Native Spirituality were present. Rachel also realised that Paul held quite a lot of attraction for her. He had a much greater depth than any male she had ever experienced before.

"This is the first time that a man's mind has attracted me as much as his body," she admitted to herself.

"I don't have time to go to that conference," Rachel tried to bolster her defences. I must be imagining that he's thinking of anything romantic. He must just want another convert to the American Indian Movement or something."

"Gran's absence would only be temporary," she told herself. "It's not like Gran would stay away forever." "You're right, Paul," she whispered to her paddling companion as the canoes made their way up the coast in the morning.

"Gran and Nigel are very close."

Paul looked at her as if trying to figure out how she felt about his other offer.

"Thanks for the warning in advance," Rachel added. "Now I've got time to psych myself up for Gran leaving if she does."

"I know you wouldn't want to stand in the way of your grandmother's happiness, Rachel."

"No, of course not. I'll just have to get used to being alone."

"You don't have to be alone, Rachel," Paul whispered. "Remember, I practice law down in Vancouver. All it will take is a phone call, and I'm available for a beautiful, intelligent, brave person like you, anytime."

"Thanks, Paul." Rachel felt her emotions churning. "I'll remember that."

"He didn't say anything about the conference," her mind mused. "Maybe he's interested in more than just turning me into an activist."

Paul knew enough not to press her any further that day.

As they came alongside one of the small fishing villages along the coast that afternoon, Rachel stared hard and did a double take at the few fishing boats tied up to mooring buoys in front of the village site. The canoes were several hundred yards offshore but the boats were clearly visible, reflecting in the bright sunlight.

"No white and grey fishboat there," Paul remarked, noting Rachel's sudden look of extreme concern.

"No, but look at that blue fishboat, Paul. It's been freshly painted, I think. And those poles. There's something florescent on them, just like the boat that picked up Nate and rammed us."

"You're right, Rachel," Paul stared at the boat in the distance intently.

"Someone's watching us from that boat with binoculars," he said.

Rachel stared. A large man could be seen outside the wheelhouse. A glint of reflected sun off metal revealed the binoculars he was staring through.

Paul pulled out the communication device from it's case in the bottom of the dugout. He buzzed Clarissa.

"Take a good look at the blue fishboat moored by the shore," he ordered.

"You're right, Paul. There's a large man staring at us with binoculars. I'm going to notify the authorities."

Clarissa turned in their direction, and slowly approached the lead canoe. Paul grabbed the boat's line as Clarissa cut the motor and drifted over to the canoe.

Paul passed the line to Rachel and pulled himself up onto the deck of the fishboat. He went into the wheelhouse.

"What's going on?" Nigel demanded.

"Take a good look at that blue fishboat by the shore, Nigel," Rachel advised. The other dugouts were now gathered around the lead canoe.

Everyone stared at the blue fishboat moored by the village. All of a sudden the figure outside the wheelhouse of the boat, reached over the side, and released the mooring line from the buoy. He went back inside the wheelhouse and the sound of the boat's motor turning over reached the canoes.

"Oh, oh, we've triggered him," Rachel warned.

"Paul," Nigel shouted. "That bastard's coming for us again. I recognize the sound of that motor. He must have been lying in wait all this time."

The paddlers in all the canoes watched in horror as the blue fishboat quickly accelerated into it's top speed and headed straight for them.

"Scatter the canoes," Nigel shouted at the top of his voice, waving his arms. "That way he can't get all of us at once."

Rachel threw the rope onto the deck of the large fishboat as Clarissa's boat motor sprang to life. The dugouts broke apart as each paddled in different directions. Clarissa's fishboat with Paul still on board leaped forward to intercept the rapidly advancing boat coming in their direction. The two boats were on a collision path with each other.

"Get ready to jump if that bastard gets by Clarissa," Nigel shouted. Rachel felt her heart pounding fiercely.

"Not again!" she thought.

Rachel and the others watched as Paul appeared on the front deck carrying a large rifle. Her heart pounded as he kneeled, braced his back against the wheelhouse and aimed the rifle.

A loud bang sounded and Paul fell backwards with the force of the shot. The blue fishboat's motor changed to a high-pitched whine. Suddenly the blue fishboat swerved away from Clarissa and the dugouts as it's owner tried to flee. Rachel realised their attacker was trying to make a run for it into one of the long Inlets on the coast.

Both fishboats quickly moved away from the dugouts. Before long both boats disappeared out of the paddler's view, but another gunshot echoed from the distance. Rachel hoped it was Paul attempting another shot and not the fellow on the blue fishboat firing.

"Look at the water," Nigel shouted.

The paddlers stared across to where the boats had been. Rachel realised that an oil slick was present in the water. It was spreading out as the wave's disbursed it.

"Paul must have hit the motor," Nigel told them. "That motor won't go very far once it runs out of whatever fluid that's leaking."

All eyes were on the distance. The canoes had regrouped themselves again and were paddling in unison after the fishboats. They paddled for about a half an hour when all of a sudden Clarissa's fishboat came into view coming towards them. She slowed and cut her motor as she neared the canoes.

Paul appeared on deck and threw the rope to Rachel. He jumped into the lead dugout and motioned the other canoes to come over.

"The fishboat's moved into Smith Inlet," he advised. "We've radioed for assistance. That boat's motor is leaking fluid and that creep can't get far. Clarissa thought she had better come back and stay with the canoes until everyone goes ashore in case that fellow isn't alone. She doesn't want to leave the dugouts without an escort vessel."

Paul was disappointed that Clarissa had called off the chase. He motioned the canoes to move towards shore.

It took close to an hour for the paddlers to get to shore and locate a cove where they could spend the night. Finally they spotted one with enough room to shelter everyone.

"Set up the tents for the night," Paul directed.

He grabbed several of the paddlers and they waded into the water and jumped back onto Clarissa's fishboat.

"Good luck," Nigel shouted as the large fishboat headed up the coast again.

"I wouldn't want to be that guy when they catch up to him," Rachel said to Gran.

The remaining paddlers set up the tents for the night and got a roaring campfire going on the small beach with some driftwood. They cooked a makeshift dinner and by the time they had eaten it was starting to get dark.

Rachel started to worry about Paul and the others as the sun disappeared behind the horizon.

"They'll be all right," Nigel advised, reading her thoughts.

Several hours later, the lights of Clarissa's fishboat came into sight. Everyone ran down to the water as Paul and the others jumped from the deck and waded in to shore. Clarissa moved the boat further out and released the anchor for the night. Rachel could tell from their expressions that they hadn't located their attacker.

"That guy must have nine lives like a cat," Paul complained as he and the others moved towards the tents. "Not a trace of him. We should have kept after him, rather than coming back."

"Clarissa did the right thing," Gran reassured Paul. "The lives of the paddlers are more important than anything else."

"Besides, he won't be going very far with that motor hit by that magnum bullet," Nigel added.

"I tried to hit him again but the bastard swerved," Paul commented."

"Don't worry, Paul. The Coast Guard and the R.C.M.P. people have planes and boats searching. They'll find the boat and that fellow in the morning, I'm sure," Nigel told him.

Paul and the others who had gone with Clarissa sat down in front of the fire. Rachel and Gran warmed up the dinner they had saved for them.

"Clarissa says to continue paddling in the morning. We've got a rendezvous with the four dugouts coming down the coast at Namu in close to a week's time. We can't afford to waste any more time looking for that fellow. She says to place someone on the boat with her at all times in case that fishboat is still capable of attacking us."

Alphonse Jack volunteered to man the gun.

"Let the Coast Guard and the R.C.M.P. locate that fishboat, Paul," Nigel advised.

The other paddlers talked for awhile and then went off to bed. Rachel, Paul, Nigel and Gran were still talking amongst themselves when the sand in front of the campfire began to swirl.

"Oh, no," Rachel cried out. "Not again!" She quickly passed out as the now all-too-familiar vortex crushed her chest unmercifully.

CHAPTER 13

Culture Resurgence

"Mother Jesus," Rachel heard as she regained consciousness. "Another Potlatch, where are we now Darling?" Rachel stared around her and forced her eyes to focus. She, Paul, Nigel and Gran were leaning against the back wall of a large cedar plank longhouse staring at a line of Hamatsas dancing in front of a painted screen.

"My God, I can't believe it," Rachel heard Gran reply as she stared at one of the dancers. "It's Herbert Martin," I'm sure. He always used that mask when he danced as a Hamatsa."

"Herbert Martin?" I questioned. "That fellow that shouted the Hamatsa cry through the streets of New Westminster and Vancouver on the way to Oakalla?"

"That's right," Gran said in amazement.

As if on cue the dancer Gran was pointing to shouted out the Hamatsa cry, "Hap, Hap."

"That's him all right," Nigel commented. "I'd recognize that cry anywhere."

I watched as Gran prodded the person next to her on the bench and asked who the Potlatch was for. The fellow didn't even flinch as Gran poked him. I realised that we were invisible and inaudible as usual in the time flashbacks. I pointed over at the person next to Paul Archer. He had a printed program in his hand.

"I'll go see if I can get one of those programs," Nigel volunteered.

"These people in the audience are dressed in fairly modern

clothes," Paul commented. "And there are both First Nations people and whites in the audience."

"Look at the Sisiutls," Gran cried. "The double-headed serpent on the cross-beams, what art work!" I followed her pointing finger. Gran was right. The craftsmanship in the longhouse was outstanding.

I glanced around. The longhouse we found ourselves in was magnificent. It was at least seventy feet long and I estimated about fifty feet wide. Four huge, decorated house posts supported the huge beams.

"What's that bird?" I asked Gran, pointing at the front posts. "That's an Oolus, Dear," Gran replied, "a supernatural bird, and that's a Grizzley Bear Crest at the bottom. A Tsunugua, a wild woman creature of the woods, is on the bottom of the back posts with Thunderbird on top."

Nigel came back clutching a program in his hand.

"These names," he commented. "James Knox, Flora Alfred-Sewid, Herbert Martin," they are the same last names we heard at that Potlatch in 1921. Is this some kind of deja vu experience?"

"No, Nigel," Gran said, staring at the program. "I know where we are now. This is Alert Bay on Cormorant Island. You remember. We spent the night in the day school building there, after the Potlatch trial. This must be the longhouse that the Alert Bay people constructed in the mid nineteen-sixties. But I heard it had burned down recently."

"What a shame," Rachel remarked as she looked at the magnificent longhouse.

"Alert Bay became an administrative and cultural centre for the Kwakiutl people in the sixties. I imagine we're attending the potlatch for the longhouse when it was put up. It was one of the first longhouses restored after the Potlatch ban was lifted in 1951. Raven must be showing us one of the things that happened in the sixties and seventies during the resurgence of the culture."

"Finally, something positive," Rachel said to Paul.

We stared back at the Hamatsas. One of the dancers was being instructed by Herbert Martin and one of the other dancers.

"The program says that this is a Potlatch given for Chief James Knox," Gran commented. "James Knox, that's the young boy that spent two months in Oakalla for dancing at the 1921 potlatch. I guess he's grown up to be a chief. And if I'm not mistaken, that's James Knox, himself teaching his younger brother Peter. I imagine Peter's being initiated into the Hamatsa Secret Society tonight."

The Hamatsas ended their dance and two fellows came out and danced the feather dance.

"That's James Sewid," I think and his friend Charlie Peters from Cape Mudge," Gran commented, looking at the program. James Sewid lived in Alert Bay most of his life. He was one of the officers of the Native Brotherhood of B. C. He was instrumental in setting up this longhouse in Alert Bay. I think his wife, Flora, was the daughter of Moses Alfred, one of the Kwakiutl people sentenced to Oakalla."

The feather dance ended and I watched James Sewid deliver a speech.

"Let us not lose our arts like we did our lands," he instructed the audience, "for if we do we shall regret it. Let us start an industry of Arts and Crafts for our people."

"We're watching the start of the Kwakwakl Arts And Crafts Organization," Gran commented.

The dancing ended about midnight. Then sandwiches, cakes and coffee were served. We watched, fascinated, as articles and small gifts of money were passed out to the older chiefs, older persons and young men.

"Imagine, these people don't have to worry about being arrested now for staging or taking part in a Potlatch," Paul commented. "It only took ninety years of protest."

"If it's 1965, First Nation's People have been able to vote in Federal Elections for five years, can now go into beer parlours and buy liquor if they wish. but look how long it took to get those rights," he added.

"Instead of attending native day schools with unqualified teachers Alert Bay students are integrated into the white school, here," Gran said.

"Unqualified teachers?" Rachel asked.

"People like retired missionaries, Dear. It was almost impossible to get certified teachers to teach in Indian schools. I believe that James Sewid's daughter Daisy, was one of the first native students in B. C. to graduate from High School after integration. Before integration, Natives were just told to go home when they reached fifteen or sixteen years old."

"Wasn't Alert Bay one of the first villages to stop sending young Indian boys to delinquent boy's correctional places?" Paul asked.

"That's right, Paul. Can you believe it. In 1963, an astonishing eighty-five Alert Bay teenagers were sent to correctional school. James Sewid and the Council here got authority to set up a special receiving home next to the R.C.M.P. station and set up the Cormorant Island Youth Guidance Committee. That helped many of our young people."

"In 1966, the Alert Bay people were given back their foreshore, I read somewhere," Paul added.

"Their foreshore, Gran?" Rachel queried.

"Yes, Rachel. The land in between the ocean and the road along the front of the village houses. In 1932, Indian Agent William Halliday grabbed the foreshore when the road was build. He leased it to the Alert Bay Shipyards for $120.00 a year, but then the government seized it and leased it to the Shipyard for three to four hundred dollars a year. It took thirty-four years of protest to get the foreshore restored to the reserve."

James Sewid made another speech that night.

"We are not treaty Indians and have not given up the ownership of B. C. to the white man," he said.

"See how our people never gave up the land claims," Paul stated. "I remember the words of James Sewid. I read his autobiography."

Rachel listened closely as she realised that the land claims question was very much on the minds of Native Peoples of B. C.. even in the fifties and sixties.

"I think the biggest problem to be solved and the most important is the land question," Paul recalled James Sewid's words as best he could. "We are not Treaty Indians on the coast and I think we should be compensated for our land. When the Europeans came here and settled, they just took all our mineral and timber and salmon and everything we rightfully owned and they have never settled it with us. We have been pounding and pounding on the doors of government because we would like to settle it so we can satisfy the minds of the Indians."

As Paul recalled the words of James Sewid, the longhouse started spinning fiercely. Rachel gasped as the four paddlers were suddenly encapsulated in the time vortex again. Her lungs felt like they were going to burst.

When she regained consciousness Rachel realised that she, Gran, Paul and Nigel were gathered around a huge campfire in the middle of a muddy road. Rain was coming down in torrents. Rachel stared at a huge carved wooden Eagle beside the fire and two solitary figures drumming on a ceremonial drum.

"That's Bill Reid," Gran told her. "The famous artist from Skidegate, on the Queen Charlotte Islands."

"I remember seeing the television newscasts of this," Nigel remarked in astonishment. "The newsreels of the logging protests on Lyall Island even reached England."

"The poor man," Rachel remarked. "He's soaking wet. And look how his hands are shaking."

"That's the Parkinson's disease that eventually took his life," Paul said. "I know. I was here as a young kid when our elders were all arrested."

"I wouldn't want to drive past that Eagle," Gran testified. Rachel and the others watched as Bill Reid and another man chanted an ancient Haida song in the pouring rain. "That's a curse," Martha McBay interpreted. "Aimed at anyone that drives through past that wooden Eagle."

"We'd better try and get out of this rain," Nigel advised. Rachel realised that all of them, including Gran, were getting absolutely drenched by the pouring, freezing rain. They moved under one of the huge first growth trees threatened by the newly made logging road. Dawn was just breaking although the heavy clouds blocked out most of the sun. In the dim light a convoy of vehicles reached the site. To Rachel's astonishment, a group of native elders got out of the cars and joined Bill Reid and the other Haida in marching around the huge fire and the eagle. The female elders were dressed in ceremonial red and black button blankets, with plastic sheets covering them in an attempt to keep off some of the rain.

Bill Reid and the other drummer chanted a different song. The elders joined in and the site rang with the echoed chants from the forests and cliffs. Suddenly the huge raindrops slowed. By the time a convoy of logging equipment and R.C.M.P. cruisers and four-wheel-drives arrived the rain had stopped completely.

The elders stood in a dignified manner completely blocking the road. Rachel watched in amazement as a senior R. C. M. P. officer approached the group and read aloud from a white, printed injunction in his hands. He told the elders that unless they moved from the road his officers would arrest them. None of the ladies moved.

"They're not going to take them into those police vehicles, are they?" Rachel asked anxiously. Some of the native elders looked like they were in their eighties or nineties.

"Watch and see," Paul told her.

The officer motioned towards his men. Determined R. C. M. P. officers moved towards the ladies. The loggers in the background climbed out of their trucks and cheered the police on. The line of native elders refused to budge.

Rachel watched in horror as one by one each of the Haida elders were seized by several officers, dragged and hauled over to waiting police vehicle and forced into the back seat.

"See how they are using non-violent, passive resistion techniques?" Paul asked Rachel.

A camera crew from a television station carefully recorded every move of the action.

"Those scenes did more to evoke public sympathy than anything else that the First Nations people did."

Finally every one of the protestors had been hauled off into the police vehicles. The vehicles moved off in a convoy. Several of the loggers appoached the still-standing large, carved Eagle and the still fiercely burning fire in the middle of the road.

"No," cried Paul as two of the loggers seized the eagle and threw it to the side of the road. The others knocked the logs in the fire over and tried to extinguish the flames with fire extinguishers. The fire was eerily difficult to put out. It put up a fierce resistance. Finally a bull-dozer was unloaded from a tractor-tailor and the remaining logs and flames were pushed aside. A cheer went up from the loggers. They jumped back into their equipment and the vehicles moved up the road towards a logging site.

"I believe the contractor doing the logging on Lyall Island suffered many delays," Paul remarked.

Suddenly the muddy site began to swirl in front of Rachel's eyes. After several excruciating minutes Rachel found herself in the middle of a room jammed full of First Nations men dressed in business suits examining papers out of the briefcases they each seemed to possess. She managed to stand up and made her way to the side of the room where Gran, Nigel, and Paul were leaning unsteadily on the wall.

"What's going on here, Gran?" Rachel asked.

"That's Frank Calder, Rachel," Gran pointed. One of the Nishga'a Tribal Council members who got elected as a member of the New Democratic Party in the 1950's when voting rights were extended to provincial First Nation's people. At the same time they were extended to Chinese and Japanese citizens of B. C. I think we must be watching a early meeting of the Nishga'a Tribal Council, sometime in the nineteen sixties. Planning land claims strategies, I imagine."

"Our mountains are getting stripped. Everything is being taken from us." Rachel turned as a man at the head of the table got up and started to address everyone furiously.

"Where my father and I hunted and trapped," he continued. "I went back there, recently. There are no trees, now. Something has to be done."

"I think that's Chief James Gosnell," Gran commented.

"We need to go to the courts," the man Gran had identified as Frank Calder stood up. "We've done enough futile lobbying for public support of our claims in this Province. I'm tired of these endless Radio talk shows and trying to educate the people of this province. Imagine, most of them think we've been dealt with more than generously."

"Won't we be on trial?" someone asked.

"It's not the Nishga'a that will be on trial," Calder stated. "It's British Justice that's will be on trial. I believe that British Justice will prevail in this country. If not the people will go to the Hague, to the heavies, the world Court, the United Nations," he said.

"I believe Calder is referring to the 1763 Proclamation by King George III," Paul explained. "The English monarch directed that the lands to the west of his existing settlements in Canada belonged to the Indians and must be extinguished by Treaty. That has been the basis of every land claim in this province from 1913 on. That both Federal and Provincial government officials failed to carry out the orders of their superior by not making treaties and that therefore title still remained with the Indians."

"Why are they all wearing business suits?" Rachel asked.

"It was part of the Nishga'a strategy, Dear," Gran replied. "Men like Frank Calder and James Gosnell were educated. They had managed to obtain higher education. Some people say they became "bicultural," that they learned how to do things in both the First Nations world and the world of the B. C. and Federal Government oppressors."

"That's right, Martha," Paul agreed. "If three piece suits, short haircuts and briefcases would help First Nations negotiators get past the stereotypical "wild beasts of the field" impression of Indi-

ans held by ignorant government officials and some members of
the legal profession then that's what would be worn."

"Then it's agreed?" Frank Calder said.

"Tom Berger is willing to take our land Claim to court. We
shall proceed?"

The men in the room jumped to their feet and person after
person gave speeches in favour of pursuing the land claim in court.

Rachel could feel the depth of the emotion in the room. Then
suddenly the walls started revolving rapidly. Rachel experienced
one severe stab of pain in her lower back and then found herself
back around the fire in front of the tents near Smith Inlet on the
coast of B. C.

"I can't believe they arrested those Native elders on the Queen
Charlottes," she gasped once she had her breath back and her eyes
focusing again.

"A lot of good it did them, Rachel," Paul advised.

"By the time of the Meares Island logging protest on the Queen
Charlottes, the Nishga'a case that we saw Frank Calder and the
others initiate was already making waves in the courts of B. C. It
wasn't long after the Meare's arrests that the courts ruled in favour
of the Haida. The judge ruled that resource extraction should stop
on Meares Island until the supreme court decided the issue of
whether Native Title had been extinguished in British Columbia.
Logging on Deer Island in Kwakiutl territory was also halted as
well as railway development on the Thompson River. Logging
preparation was also stopped in Gitksan Wet'suwet'en Territory.
That's the power of non-violent protests, and properly prepared
litigation, like I've been telling you."

"The Calder case made the governments more receptive to
negotiating treaties, Paul?" Rachel asked. "I know I should know
these things but I'm afraid I was busy learning subjects like statis-
tics and research design, instead."

"Calder v. Attorney-General of B. C. (1974) was the main case
that sent Federal politicians scurrying, Rachel," Paul answered. "It
was the claim put forth in 1964 by the Nishga'a for their old

territories on the basis of Indian Title from aboriginal use and occupation. When Mr. Justice Hill of the Supreme Court of Canada held that the title was still good today, the Feds announced that they intended to settle native land claims all across Canada where no treaties had been made."

"There was a setback, though," Paul advised. "None of us could believe it when Justice Allan McEarchern, the Chief Justice of the Supreme Court of B. C., in the Delgamuukw v. The Queen (1991) appeal ruled that the Gitskan and Wet'suwet'en hereditary chiefs were too primitive to have property rights."

"But that setback has been overruled now, by Chief Justice Lamer of the Supreme Court of Canada who ruled that Justice McEarchern erred in the Delgamuukw decision and threw the decision out of court in Dec. 1997," Paul said in triumph. "And if we can just manage to get our dugouts to Bella Bella to show solidarity, there's a good chance that the remaining forty-four B. C. land claims will be decided in treaty negotiations like Justice Lamer recommended."

CHAPTER 14

Run For The Finish

The flotilla of dugout canoes camped on their small beach for three days after the thwarted attack. The R.C.M.P. and Coast Guard still had not located the fishboat that had charged at them before Smith's Inlet.

"Where could that man have gone?" Rachel questioned Gran.

"There's so many coves in these inlets, Dear," Gran sighed, "and uninhabited islands."

"Something is really weird the way that guy managed to disappear so fast," Paul added. "He must have stopped and managed to slow the leakage from that motor when Clarissa turned back. Maybe he was somehow able to reach full speed and made a run for it up the coast instead of continuing up Smith Inlet."

"That's not very comforting, Paul," Rachel said. "He might still be out there waiting for an opportunity to strike again. He might even be above Namu, waiting to ambush the canoes coming down the coast to join us, if he knows anything about them."

"That's a frightening possibility, Rachel."

"The other canoes have an escort vessel and it's equipped with a magnum rifle, too," Clarissa told them. We'll go at dawn, tomorrow."

"I hope that guy is not going to come for us again," Rachel stated.

"If he does we'll be ready for him. Alphonse Jack is going to position himself on the front deck with that magnum rifle loaded and pointed this time. Alphonse is hoping the guy is going to "make his day.""

Rachel smiled at the short, heavy-set, Heiltsuk woman. She could hear the determination in her voice. The next morning, Gran conducted the cleansing rituals in the dark. The flotilla set out at the break of day towards Namu, their paddlers pulling through the water with grim determination.

Rachel realised that the easy attunement with the sea and nature attained by the paddlers on the journey was now gone. In it's place was an intense anxiety that the maniac determined to stop the "Voyage of Solidarity" would stage another attack. As the paddlers came upon every cove and possible hiding spot along the coast Rachel felt the hair on the back of her neck rise in anticipation of skullduggery. But this time nothing happened.

By the time the afternoon was upon them they had cleared Smith Sound and had Calvert Island in sight in the distance.

It was a sunny day with only a light chop on the water.

"Look at the Orcas," Paul shouted.

Rachel couldn't believe it. A pod of five black and white killer whales were leaping out of the water ahead of the canoes.

"Another omen," Martha McBay shouted. "They're headed straight for Namu. We'll make it there for sure."

Gran was right. Nothing out of the ordinary happened for the next three days. They reached the beach at Namu precisely as the setting sun went behind the horizon.

The next morning Rachel and the others waited on the shore as the four dugout canoes travelling together down from Prince Rupert came into sight. Leading the canoes was the Raven Song canoe of the Tsimshian people carrying it's fourteen paddlers. The Haisla canoe from Kitimat was next, followed by the canoe of the Haida people, and the Nuxult canoe.

Rachel gasped as the paddlers in the canoes were wearing their finest regalia. In the Tsimshian canoe, Raven Song, a young Tsimshian stood at attention in the front of the boat holding his carved wooden stick with Eagle at the top. A dancer wearing a carved Bear mask and a fur robe danced ceremoniously in the front of the Haisla canoe. The Haida warriors were all dressed in their finest red and black button blankets. The elegantly attired paddlers proudly wearing Chilkat blankets in the Nuxult canoe from Bella Coola chanted an ancient song in unison.

Emotion choked Rachel's throat as all four canoes lined up in front of the beached dugouts that had made their way up the Coast and raised their paddles in salute. One by one chanters in the canoes requested permission to come ashore. Gran answered each one and a huge yell of triumph sounded as the paddlers from up the coast came onto the shore to be hugged and greeted by the paddlers from down the coast.

The next morning, the chiefs of the Canoe Societies arrived in boats of all kind. and space was made for them in each dugout.

Rachel realised that any threat of attack should now be gone as the number of boats moving to Bella Bella along with the canoes was enough to discourage even the most foolhardy attacker.

The flotilla was quite a sight that day as paddlers practiced their final entry procedures. Everyone wore their finest regalia as Nigel Kent drilled all the paddlers over and over again in the ritual of the entrance of the flotilla into Bella Bella. He wouldn't stop until everything was absolutely perfect.

The morning after special ceremonies the entire flotilla took to the water. The sun was shining, the wind was low, and the canoes were expected to be in Bella Bella in approximately five hours.

Martha McBay felt choked with emotion as Nigel Kent took off behind the paddlers in a small float plane. He was going ahead to take command of the film crew that was on the scene in Bella Bella to record the dugouts coming in for their welcome by the waiting crowd.

Nigel flew low over the canoes several times. Martha knew he was hoping to get a shot of all the canoes lined up together as they raced towards their final destination.

"Clarissa directed a media blitz at the last moment, Rachel," Paul told her. "They'll be television crews and reporters from all over Canada as well as Nigel to record the success of the "Voyage of Solidarity.""

When the lead canoe turned into the passage between Hunter Island and Bella Bella, Rachel McBay gave a huge sigh of relief. She had been watching both shorelines intently, afraid that their unknown attacker was going to make a final move to stop the successful completion of the journey.

As the lead canoe came close to the shore in the passage an unusual happening occurred. A large, black raven came out to the canoe from the thick woods on Hunter Island and gave it's deep-throated cry several times over the paddler's heads.

"I don't like that, Paul," Martha McBay told the dugout coordinator. "That raven was trying to tell us something."

"You're right Martha," he answered. "Keep your eyes open," he warned the paddlers. "But whatever happens I imagine we've got enough escort boats to handle it. Surely nothing can stop us now!"

As they reached the entrance to the harbor the canoes moved abreast of each other and travelled in unison for the last nautical mile. An incoming high tide was allowing the canoes to surge right into the shore with a minimum of effort. Martha McBay and the other tribal chanters broke into a moving chant of thanks and triumph as the paddlers approached the shore. About fifty feet from shore the paddlers slowed the canoes and their carved and decorated paddles were thrust high in the air in unison as a final salute to the throngs of First Nation's peoples lining the shore.

Rachel couldn't believe the thousands of First Nations people lining the shore and going wild. Drums and whistles sounded as dancers from the different Nations celebrated on shore. Everyone celebrated for several minutes and then suddenly the Chief of Bella Bella raised his arm in the air with his ceremonial talking stick. All celebrating ceased and the crowd stood motionless waiting in anticipation.

Martha McBay stood and chanted the first request for permission to come ashore. The sound of the Chief of Bella Bella returning her greetings and giving permission to disembark came through the air. Paul Archer turned towards Rachel to give her a hug of triumph.

"There's even more people that we had at Qatuwas," he shouted.

"Oh My God," Rachel cried out as she turned and looked past Paul out into the way they had come. Her heart stood still as she found herself staring at a bright blue fishboat drifting ominously towards everyone from the distance.

"It's that boat again but there's no motor sound," she cried out to Paul.

"Christ, you're right, Rachel! That boat is drifting right towards us on the tide," Paul answered. "We've got to find out what's going on."

Suddenly the chanting on the shoreline was broken by the sound of a boat motor starting up.

"It's Clarissa," Rachel shouted. "Thank God she's seen that boat, too. Imagine, right in the middle of the welcoming ceremonies."

Clarissa slowly made her way over to Paul's canoe. The crowd on shore wondered what was going on. The rest of the chanters stood silently, now staring out at the silent, blue fishboat drifting towards them in the distance.

"Come along, Rachel," Paul shouted. He grabbed onto Clarissa's deck and helped Rachel pull herself on board. He and Alphonse Jack jumped up behind her. All of them were wearing traditional cedar bark vests and hats. They had to remove the hats to fit into the wheelhouse with Clarissa.

"We've got to intercept that boat," Paul told Clarissa. "It looks disabled but we can't be sure."

Clarissa nodded.

"Tell the chanter in the second canoe to go on with the ceremonies," she directed. Paul went out and ordered the chanter to proceed. Alphonse Jack grabbed the magnum rifle and turned towards the door.

"Don't shoot until we get closer," Paul warned. Alphonse nodded and moved out in front of the wheelhouse. Clarissa slowly backed away from the dugouts and then sped up to intercept the fishboat.

"Go tell Alphonse not to fire, Paul," she suddenly decided.

"There's something very odd about this." Rachel could feel it herself. Something didn't seem right.

It took Clarissa only a few minutes to pull slowly up to the drifting fishboat. Rachel stood in the open door of the wheelhouse and searched the vessel with her eyes.

"There doesn't seem to be anyone on board," Rachel told Clarissa.

"Don't be too sure, Rachel," Clarissa advised.

Clarissa moved up slowly against the boat. Paul leaped onto the deck of the old fishboat. He attached a heavy rope to a ring in front of the wheelhouse and threw the rope over to Alphonse Jack. He moved cautiously towards the wheelhouse. No one seemed to be in it or on the boat.

"Oh, Jesus," he shouted suddenly and leaped back from the wheelhouse.

"Dynamite," he shouted to Alphonse Jack.

"Dynamite," Alphonse relayed to Clarissa. "In the wheelhouse. Attached to wires."

"Secure that rope," Clarissa yelled to Alphonse. "At the back of my boat, Tell Paul to get off that floating bomb."

"Get out of there, Man!" Alphonse Jack yelled. Paul clambered back aboard.

"There's a detonator attached to wires." Paul gasped. "And I could hear loud ticking through the door of the wheelhouse. There must be some kind of timer. Maybe I should go back and try to disarm the mechanism."

"No, Paul. The door to the wheelhouse might be rigged," Clarissa decided.

"We're probably running out of time," Paul warned.

Rachel looked back towards shore. The fishboats were both drifting on the tide surge now. They were less than three hundred feet from the canoes and the people on shore. It looked like the canoes were still being ceremoniously brought to shore.

"There's at least twenty sticks of dynamite in that wheelhouse," Paul told Clarissa. "Enough to blow up all the canoes," he added.

Clarissa made her mind up on the spot. "We've got to get that boat away from the canoes and people on shore," she gasped.

"Get ready to release that rope when I give the order," Clarissa yelled at Alphonse Jack. He picked up an axe and hovered over the rope. Clarissa started the motor and moved out into the harbor away from the shore. The blue fishboat followed obediently behind.

Clarissa flipped a switch and spoke into her marine radio.

"SOS," she announced. "Anyone picking up this broadcast. Tell the Chief to stop the proceedings right now," she ordered. "The wheelhouse of that blue fishboat is filled with dynamite. Get everyone off the beach immediately."

Rachel stared at the old boat in horror. Any moment she knew the boat was going to explode and send them all into another world. Clarissa pushed the throttle full way in and her fishboat surged ahead.

It seemed an eternity as Clarissa roared away from Bella Bella and towards Hunter Island.

"This will have to do," she shouted after sixty seconds of running full out. "Let the rope go," she yelled to Alphonse Jack. He chopped the rope off with the axe and the old fishboat parted company. It kept moving towards Hunter Island in the distance. Clarissa turned her fishboat sharply and headed away from the old blue boat. She pushed the throttle in and roared off.

Within less than a minute there was a deafening explosion. Rachel felt herself hurled to the floor with Paul and Clarissa. She felt excruciating pain in her right ear and her left ear was ringing something fierce. Shattered glass was scattered all over them. Miraculously the fishboat they were on continued full speed ahead. A fierce wind surged at Rachel through the broken windows. She tried to focus her eyes as Clarissa attempted to drag herself to her feet. Suddenly the boat surge stopped as Clarissa did something to the controls.

"Rachel, there's blood flowing from your ear," Paul's voice sounded extremely anxious. Rachel reached up and felt a wet stickiness. She glanced at her hand. Blood was on it.

"Don't worry," she said to Paul. "It's likely just a broken eardrum. We should get off so lightly!" Tears of gratitude formed in Rachel's eyes as she realised no one other than herself had been seriously injured.

"The ancestors must have been watching over us!" Paul cried out.

The fishboat kept drifting in the water.

"Alphonse?" Clarissa yelled as Paul held Rachel anxiously in his arms.

"I'm all right," all six feet four of Alphonse Jack came into the wheelhouse.

All of them staggered out onto the deck. Gear was scattered everywhere. Clarissa's boat looked like a hurricane had roared over it.

"Look at the old fishboat," Alphonse Jack shouted. They all turned. The boat was still partially floating, several hundred yards from them. It was unrecognizable. Whatever was left of the boat was burning fiercely on the surface of the water. All kinds of debris from the boat was floating all around.

"Go in closer," Paul advised Clarissa.

"Whatever for?" she questioned.

"The debris," he answered. "Maybe there's something that will help us identify that bastard? Imagine, he was going to blow up everybody."

"Good idea," Clarissa answered. "Are you going to be all right, Rachel? Or should we take you to a hospital right away."

"I think it's just a broken eardrum," Rachel managed, checking herself out. "In my right ear." Rachel decided not to tell Clarissa about her dizziness and extreme pain.

"Go have a look at the debris," she urged Clarissa. "Anything that might help us learn who that maniac is."

Paul held Rachel steady as Clarissa crunched her way over the broken glass back into the wheelhouse. The motor coughed a bit but then went into it's customary roar. Clarissa turned the boat towards the flaming wreckage and slowly moved towards it. As she cruised over to start of the debris Paul and Alphonse began fishing out whatever they could grab with long poles.

Rachel sat on the deck keeping her dizziness and pain to herself for quite a while as Clarissa moved the boat slowly through the debris.

"I can't complain," she told herself. "This might be our only chance to find out who Nate Archer's murderer is. And besides, I don't want to look like a wimp in front of Paul."

"This should do it," Rachel felt great relief as she heard Paul shout for Clarissa. She focused her eyes in his direction. Paul had pulled up a bright orange object from the ocean.

Clarissa came out of the wheelhouse and stared at the object. It was a life jacket, somehow looking completely unscathed from the explosion except for the water dripping from it.

"The 'Malcolm Jay,'" Paul pronounced, reading the ship's name proudly emblazoned on the jacket.

"I think we had better get Rachel to a hospital," Clarissa announced. "And I'm sure the R.C.M.P. will want to pay a visit to the owner of the "Malcolm Jay." Clarissa moved back into the wheelhouse and the boat moved off towards the Bella Bella Harbor. Rachel could see Clarissa pick up the marine radio and speak into it as the boat rushed along.

"I guess she's alerting the R.C.M.P.," Paul said as he held Rachel close on the deck.

CHAPTER 15

Another Aftermath

Rachel was wheeled into the operating room as soon as the doctor in the Emergency Ward took a look at her ear.

"She might lose the hearing in her right ear," he warned Clarissa as the nurses wheeled her stretcher into the operating room. That was the last thing Rachel heard as she lost consciousness.

When she regained consciousness in a hospital room several hours later Gran and Nigel rushed over to her. Paul was standing quietly behind them.

"They've got him, Dear," Rachel struggled to make sense of her grandmother's words as she returned to consciousness.

"The R.C.M.P. phoned Clarissa and she just called me, Rachel," Paul explained as he went over to Rachel's side, picked up her hand and kissed it gently.

"You should have told me you were in great pain," he said accusingly.

"And miss a chance to find out who Nate's murderer was," Rachel answered. "Who was he, does anyone know?"

"The Malcolm Jay's owner is a fellow named Michael McNight," Nigel said excitedly. "Some of the crowd on shore saw him towing the fishboat before it drifted towards us. He was using the little zodiac he carried on the back. Others told the R.C.M.P. that he'd rushed to the float plane in the harbor from the zodiac as it landed. Cops down the coast pulled him off the plane just a couple of hours ago. When the float plane landed at New Westminster, near Vancouver."

"That's wonderful," Rachel was staring into Paul's eyes. He was giving her full eye contact.

"McNight's a crazy fisherman, Rachel," Nigel added. 'And, you're going to be all right, by the way, Darling. The doctor says he thinks your right eardrum will heal completely."

Rachel felt great relief at Nigel's words as she put one of her hands on her bandaged ear. The other remained in Paul's warm grasp.

"McNight's sons are named Malcolm and Jay," Nigel continued. "McNight, himself, went completely insane, according to the R.C.M.P. When the motor of his fishboat blew up. Seems that Paul's bullet did strike the motor. McNight kept the Malcolm Jay going that night, all the way to the tip of Hunter Island. By adding oil every so often. But I guess the motor overheated, anyway."

"Why didn't the search boats or plane spot him?" Rachel questioned. "He must have been lurking near here for days."

"Apparently McNight kept going under cover of darkness," Paul explained. "He pulled the boat under some blown down trees in a small bay, felled some more small evergreens onto it and camouflaged the vessel. Used his small zodiac and motor from the back of the fishboat to go and get motor parts in Bella Bella. Tried to repair the motor."

"When he realised the motor was beyond repair he must have thought of filling the wheelhouse with dynamite and towing the Malcolm Jay into the harbor, here, the day we arrived. They think he was going to set off the blast with a remote when the tide gave him the opportunity to use a timer instead."

"The tide gave him a hand?"

"That's right, Darling."

Rachel's heart pounded. Paul had never called her that before.

"The crowd on shore were all so intent on watching the arriving canoes no one thought anything when they saw him towing the fishboat from way behind us," Paul continued. "We were all watching the shore. McNight brought the fishboat in far enough for the tide to take it the rest of the way. He released the boat and brought his zodiac into Bella Bella Harbor. Got on the morning flight to Vancouver. He would have likely got away with everything if only we hadn't fished up that life jacket, thanks to you giving us the time to locate it."

"Why did he do it?" Rachel questioned. "And kill Nate?" she gasped.

"He claims that Nate was killed in a struggle, Rachel. Like you thought, Nate tried to stop him from attacking our dugout off Chemainus."

"Imagine, that man blamed Indians for depleting the salmon stocks, Dear," Gran told her. "Apparently he's slowly been going bankrupt for years, like the rest of us, as the salmon runs have declined. He figured if First Nations people were given more of the salmon allotments as a result of Treaty settlements he would be finished for sure."

"When his motor blew up, he went into a psychotic rage," Nigel added. "The R.C.M.P. aren't even sure if he's sane enough to stand trial. It took six of them to subdue him once they pulled him from the float plane."

"Then he was acting alone after all?" Rachel queried.

"They're not sure, Dear. A large sum of money was on McNight as they caught up to him. Over one hundred thousand dollars. The R.C.M.P. are trying to track down where he got it from."

"This never ends!" Rachel felt her head spin as she tried to make sense of the circumstances.

"Rachel, how do you feel, Dear?" Gran asked, anxiety in her voice.

"I'm all right, Gran. Actually, I feel better than I have for a long time. With the murderer in a secure place, at least," she added. "It's like a weight has been lifted off my shoulders."

"Your grandmother has agreed to become my wife, Rachel," Nigel announced proudly, putting his arm around Martha McBay's shoulders.

Rachel smiled warmly as Gran flashed an absolutely exquisite ring at her.

"That's marvellous, Gran!"

Both Martha McBay and Nigel Kent looked enormously relieved.

"How do you feel about a trip to Tahiti?" Nigel demanded. "We're going to hold the wedding on the shore of the blue lagoon at Bora Bora. Martha wants you to stand up for her. Paul is coming along as my "Best Man."

"Sounds delightful," Rachel laughed. "By the way, Paul, will you make reservations for me at the 'Indigenous Warrior's Conference,' in Oregon, in late September?"

"I'd be delighted, Darling."

"Indigenous Warrior's Conference, Dear?" Martha McBay repeated in amazement. "Isn't that a little out of your line?"

"Not anymore, Gran," Rachel decided, the events of the past two months weighing heavily on her mind. "Not anymore."

9 780738 812014